Timber Trail Riders

The Luck of Black Diamond

by Michael Murray

illustrated by
Olindo Giacomini
and Arnie Kohn

A SUNNY SAUNDERS STORY

WHITMAN PUBLISHING COMPANY • Racine, Wisconsin

Copyright © 1963, by
WHITMAN PUBLISHING COMPANY
Printed in the U.S.A. by
WESTERN PRINTING AND LITHOGRAPHING COMPANY

Contents

1. Quicksand!   9
2. Dream Horse   25
3. The First Ride   40
4. "Horses Are Tops!"   58
5. Four-Legged Bully   74
6. The "Lights"   85
7. Put to the Test   97
8. A Present for Sunny   115
9. The Contest   132
10. Uncle Joe's Bombshell   148
11. Diamond Takes a Chance   164
12. Sudden Ending   180
13. Big Plans   193
14. Ruth Meets Diamond   206
15. Sunny's Sacrifice   221
16. The Worst Possible Time   237
17. The All-Important Choice   255
18. The Real Winner   273

1   *Quicksand!*

Not a horse of any variety was left for them. Brian's mother had been so uncertain about having a car that he had not telephoned for reservations.

"It's a shame," he told Sunny. "Your first trip out."

Sunny was not going to let him know how disappointed she really was. "Oh, it gives you a chance to show me around Trot Inn."

The place had no resemblance to Timber Trail Farm where she rode in Illinois, but then, much in Colorado was different. Instead of woodsy greenery close at hand, you looked into distance. Open rolling land, often sun-scorched though it was only early July, led your eyes on to the mountains. Rounded foothills in the foreground were backed by mountain ranges rising to the jagged, snowy peaks of the Continental Divide.

Yes, they had told her, there was real snow up there. Her uncle had driven her over a high pass and shown her great banks of it, melting and parting at the top of the land so some rivulets flowed west to end in the Pacific Ocean, and on the other side east to the Atlantic Ocean. They had been indeed on the top of the world.

Even here at Brian's riding ranch, they were a mile above sea level. That was part of what made Colorado different and exhilarating.

"There isn't much to show with all the riders gone." Brian shrugged. "Just the stable. Maybe a few boarder horses are not in use. Over there is the ring—back of that sort of clubhouse building."

They were standing beside a big, open stable door, with a mounting block beside it. Cars were parked all around, blocking much of the clubhouse from view. Since his friends had promised to take them home, Brian's mother had already driven away.

Off to one side was the owner's private residence, and between that and the stable a hard-packed lane looked like a wonderful start for a ride. But, not today!

"Shall we go see the horses that are still in?" she suggested.

But Brian had seen something exciting down the lane. "Hurry. We'll open the gate for him."

Now Sunny, too, saw the powerful, black horse racing at pounding speed toward them. Fury boiled in her. What a horrible way for a rider to bring in his horse! She was certain the beautiful creature was not running away. The crazy rider was obviously urging him on. If this was the way they rode around Brian's stable, she hoped her uncle could find her another place.

They were not the only ones observing the rider. Mr. Donald, the owner of Trot Inn, whom Sunny had just met, and a second man were running toward the gate after Brian. Sunny followed.

The rider shouted as soon as he could possibly make himself heard. "There's a cow in the quicksand. Sinking fast."

The anger in Mr. Donald's face faded to alarm. "Where?"

Brian had already worked a wire loop over a post,

and the men helped him release the pole holding the gate wires. They swung it around, clearing a path as the black horse galloped up, coming to an instant stop beside the men. The rider managed to keep his seat and still talk. "Just a few yards below the ridge."

Mr. Donald wheeled on his helper. "The key's in the pickup, Rod, isn't it? Get a rope, will you?"

"Do we need boards or can we find enough stuff down there?"

"Let's not waste time looking here. I'll get the pickup started."

Sunny had eyes only for the excited creature, stopped so abruptly out of a bolting race. Any other spirited horse she'd known would be dancing like crazy. This one acted as if he knew there had been a vital need for him to supply speed, and that now it was the humans' turn to act.

Mr. Donald, returning with the pickup, cast a sharp look at the wet, quivering animal. "Put him in a box stall," he ordered the rider. "Put a blanket on him and I'll rub him down as soon as I get back."

Brian begged, "Please, Mr. Donald, can't Sunny

and I ride down in the back of the pickup?"

"If you get in quick," he agreed, his eyes on his helper, Rod, coming on the run.

Brian and Sunny clambered in with a care for nothing but haste. The pickup had last been used in hauling manure, but that did not matter now.

"Hang on tight," Mr. Donald warned, as Rod flung himself into the front seat, and they went rattling down the lane.

The ride ended almost as quickly as it started. The lane, following a barbed-wire fence, crossed the side of a big pasture filled with cottonwood trees. In less than half a mile they came to the creek, where the riding group was waiting for them.

"She's still making it," a boy shouted, pointing down the creek.

Mr. Donald and Rod wasted no time in words. Brian and Sunny jumped out of the pickup and raced after them.

"Get back, get back," Mr. Donald shouted to the ring of dismounted riders standing at the edge of the creek, which widened at this point.

Sunny caught glimpses of the desperate cow's head and her entangled, scrambling feet as she struggled to climb out of mud-churned water. Rod had his rope worked into a lasso and ran forward whirling it. Steadying himself, he tossed it with expert skill at the cow's head.

"You've caught the horns," Mr. Donald crowed with joy.

But for a heartsick moment it looked as if the cow's mad struggles might dislodge the rope as Rod eased back his line. No! It held. Held!

Several of the older boys joined Rod and Mr. Donald in pulling, slowly, carefully, giving the frantic animal enough forward leverage so she could clamber out of the sucking sand. Then she lay down exhausted on the bank.

"Get back. Get back," Mr. Donald shooed everyone away. "Give her air." He bent over and studied the labored breathing. "She'll make it," he declared. "We got her in time but it's a wonder she didn't sink."

Some boys spoke up eagerly. "We did just what Doug told us to. We shoved in all the logs and big boughs we could find. We couldn't find enough big ones."

Rod stroked the cow's bleeding back gently. "They sure scratched her up."

Mr. Donald beamed at the group. "All the same, boys, it's probably what saved her."

A girl pushed forward. "It wasn't just the boys that did it, Mr. Donald. Marley found the biggest log of all."

"Good for you, Marley! And I see you riders did remember your reins." He looked back at the horses, some upset by the excitement, some taking greedy advantage of an unexpected chance to crop tender green leaves from low branches where reins were looped. Not a horse had run off.

"You'd better get going," Rod reminded them, "if you want to get in a ride before your families start calling for you."

Jointly the group moved toward their mounts. Kristy discovered her horse had stepped on a trailing rein and broken it. Mr. Donald managed to make a temporary repair, chiding her for not having knotted it properly out of danger as the others had.

As the riders began passing through a wire gate along the bridle path, Mr. Donald suddenly halted them.

"Wait. I believe if enough of you help lift, we can get old Molly in the pickup. She can get better care up at the barn."

The exhausted cow, always a gentle, patient creature, offered no resistance. The pickup was backed close to her, and in a few minutes they had her penned in with her head tied forward.

"She's safer roped though I doubt if we need to." Mr. Donald gave a last reassuring pat to Molly and climbed into the driver's seat. Rod knelt on the seat beside him, facing backward to watch her.

"You kids can walk up all right." Mr. Donald remembered Brian and Sunny enough to tell them that without further concern.

The couple watched the pickup start up the lane and the riders straggle off along the bridle path. As they closed the pasture gate behind them, Sunny looked over where the cow had been sinking. The flow of water was clearing away the muddiness, yet even in the middle, the current was not deep. Cherry Creek wasn't much of a stream.

She commented, "I guess if Denver hadn't started next to this creek no one would ever know it exists."

Brian laughed. "You've got it all mixed up. If Cherry Creek had not been here, a city like Denver would never have existed."

"This little bit of water!" Sunny did not believe him.

"You've no idea what water meant in the early West. Still does for that matter. And a lot more flows underground here than on top. That's why there's quicksand."

Sunny studied the scene of Molly's pitiful struggles. "With a place that bad I think it's terrible nobody fenced it off."

Brian shook his head. "You still don't understand. Quicksand isn't some special kind of dangerous gravel. It's the underground water that is always changing the sand around, making hollow places or whatever it is sucks things under. They claim a whole engine once disappeared around these parts and nobody ever saw it again. Railway tracks used to come out this way."

"A whole engine of a train! Do you think I'm that big a greenhorn?" Sunny laughed.

"You saw what happened to old Molly. She's been around this pasture for years. Used the creek often for a drink."

Sunny considered the stream again. The projecting ends of the logs and boughs they had tried to push under Molly were becoming a sort of island as the water washed the sand away and swirled around the mound. Nothing else warned of danger.

Brian said, "Black Diamond—you saw that horse Doug rode up to the stable?"

Had she! Oh, but that was a horse! Everything in her had gone out to him.

Brian continued, "The story is that he was in quicksand once up to his ears. Nobody can vouch for it but the old fellow sure stays away from it. He can tell it every time."

"How?" Sunny asked excitedly.

"Horse sense. I've watched him put his head way

low and sort of sniff. Maybe its smell does it. Anyway no rider ever crosses if Diamond says no."

"Tell me more about him," Sunny begged.

"He's sure the horse everyone wants. I've been lucky enough to get him a few times. You never have to urge that horse. Let's go up and see him. The boss was sure worried over the shape he was in. But Doug's riding saved old Molly. Gary told me by the time we got there she was sucked in a lot farther than when Doug left."

The pity, though, if that magnificent horse had to pay for saving a cow! "I know he had reason but that boy did ride like crazy. Still I've seen lots of horses more lathered up. They're that way in no time back home."

"Maybe it's your humidity. A horse ridden correctly out here doesn't get all foamy."

Sunny walked faster, impatient. "Hurry. I hope he's all right."

They found the front of the stable deserted. Brian told her, "We're not made welcome back beyond that haystack. The corrals and feed racks are on that side."

He motioned to the right. "The cows—what few they have—are kept on this side. Look, there's Doug over with Rod. I expect he rates since he brought the warning."

"Can't we go over just long enough to see how Molly is? She might like this." Sunny pulled a carrot out of her pocket and displayed it.

Brian looked about doubtfully. "It's so quiet maybe we won't be in the way."

He did not take the liberty of opening any gates, but Sunny was as agile as he was in swinging legs accoutered for riding over pole fences. The fences were worn smooth, the bark nibbled off by four-footed creatures or rubbed away by two-legged intruders.

"They never mind us getting up here to look on," Brian explained, "but let's go on down and see about Molly."

The cow was in the far corral and on her feet, though still shaky. Rod was washing her sore spots with a healing disinfectant. Once it stung and she wriggled that rear end, but mostly she seemed to be enjoying Rod's care. Discovering that Sunny had a carrot for her, she approved of more humans around. Next she indicated a second carrot would be even more welcome.

Sunny did have two more in her pockets, but she was not forgetting the black beauty. Maybe he liked carrots, too.

Molly, failing to secure more treats, lost interest fast. She was tired, and glad to be led over to some straw, where she stretched out gratefully.

"Come on," said Rod. "We'll let Molly get some sleep. She had a narrow escape but she'll be all right. She's a good milker and it would have been a shame to lose her."

Sunny, recalling the nibbling lips that had taken the carrot so sweetly, thought it would have been a shame for more than milking reasons.

"How's Diamond?" Brian asked Doug.

"Mr. Donald's taking care of him. I did what I could but I was in the way in the stall after the boss went to work. Let's go in and see what he thinks about him now."

Brian agreed readily, "Let's."

Sunny needed no encouragement. As she stepped

ahead in her eagerness, Brian noticed her britches. "I should have warned you about the bottom of that pickup."

Sunny slowed to give him a smile. "Do you think I would have missed all the excitement at the creek?" However she took in the extent of the stains with growing soberness. "Aunt Julia will be horrified." Then she added cheerfully, "I'll just have to get them in the washing machine before she sees them."

Brian laughed. "You're a good sport. My sister, Carla, would be so hold-her-nose at the source she'd be about sick."

"If only it doesn't come off on the car seats going home. Brian, we must remember to sit on newspapers."

"Then you'll keep out of trouble all around. You're smart, Sunny," offered Doug.

Their praise brought a happy glow to Sunny. The two were so obviously popular leaders that their approval would mean much to her standing in a new group. As a friend of Brian's family, Uncle Joe had not left Brian any choice about taking his visiting niece out with him, and she was grateful he was not finding it too much of a chore.

Entering the stable, Brian motioned to an archway at the right. Box stalls lined each side of a long passageway. Only a few were occupied, and Sunny gave these horses scant attention as she sought for her black beauty.

Toward the end of the wing, they met Mr. Donald coming out of a stall. He nodded reassuringly to their anxious looks and reported with a tired smile, "I don't believe much harm was done. He was taken care of quickly and covered up well. Doug, you did exactly right. He may be some lame tomorrow but that's to be expected."

Sunny peered inside the stall. The horse was obviously weary, but his drooping head came up at their approach. His neck arched proudly as he welcomed them.

Sunny held out a carrot. Black Diamond plainly was eager for it, but he reached with polite delicacy, showing his big white teeth enough and no more. He took it from her hand with gentle lips.

"Oh, you love! You love!" sang through Sunny,

but she kept her delight bottled inside her. She did not want the boys to scorn her for a sentimental idiot. She wanted their good opinion.

"I don't suppose anyone can ride him tomorrow, can they?" she commented as they walked out.

"I doubt it," Brian agreed. "Though plenty will want to."

Sunny wondered if she would ever be able to have a turn. She would gladly have spent the rest of her time today just being near the horse, but the first day she must stay with Brian, not have ideas of her own.

The boys wanted to toss horseshoes at a stake. It was fun, but it would have been more fun inside the stable. However, she was pleased to make some lucky tosses, enough to offer competition without actually winning, so she was in good standing when the riders returned, and she was introduced around as a desirable addition to the group.

2 *Dream Horse*

Sunny had no memory of her grandfather, but her grandmother was very much alive. Nearly twenty years ago, this lively individual had spent a winter in Paris and returned with gesturing hands and a consuming desire for what seemed French to her.

She bought a house with great bleak rooms that nobody else wanted, because it reminded her of the house where she had stayed on the Left Bank. The checkered covers at a tiny café on an island in the Seine had so entranced her that there were no more white or even plain-colored tablecloths in her home.

Mere Odette, as she insisted on being called, had bought half curtains, café style, for the dining room, but the gay window coverings she had admired in another setting were lost in the tall windows, and visitors merely wished there had been enough material to cover the bare top parts.

Sunny's mother's older sister, Julia, and her brother, Joe, lived with *Mere* Odette. Sunny could never decide if her aunt and uncle went along with their mother's fantastic notions because it was easier to agree with her or because they had so few ideas of their own to offer in competition.

Sunny herself found only one fault with *Mere* Odette. She did not appreciate horses. But Uncle Joe made up for her. Horses were his one real enthusiasm. If there was something Aunt Julia cared about deeply, Sunny had yet to discover it, unless it was order in any form.

Fortunately the gaunt old house, in its spaciousness, encouraged order. *Mere* Odette fluttered around, never putting anything back where she picked it up, but Aunt Julia replaced things equally fast.

Sunny's mother had warned her she must be careful not to worry her Aunt Julia with her sometimes careless habits, but Sunny had found this no problem. The big drawers in her chiffonier swallowed all her belongings out of sight. Aunt Julia was too polite to look inside, so her room passed as tidy. Nothing in the rest of the big old house tempted her to bother with it. She even began to have a little sympathy with Aunt Julia.

For one thing, *Mere* Odette had splurged on copper utensils of all shapes and sizes. Plate rails and deep shelves were filled with them, and in spite of Aunt Julia's loyal efforts to keep them brightly burnished they remained dark and uninteresting.

It was Sunny's first visit to her Denver relatives. Two years before her family had motored to the west coast, but they paused in Denver very briefly. Usually the relatives visited in Illinois. They had come individually several times, but only for short stays, and this six weeks' visit was Sunny's first opportunity to become really acquainted.

The first week there had been much to see and learn. Sunny had been well entertained, but now she had looked at a black horse, and her interest in everything else faded. *Mere* Odette and Aunt Julia both had ideas about Sunday procedure, but Sunny did hope she could persuade Uncle Joe to sneak in a trip to Trot Inn. She had told him of the excitement yesterday, and he, too, was concerned about its effects on Black Diamond.

"I know the horse well," he said.

Uncle Joe had lost a leg in action in World War II. Although he now had an artificial limb, riding had been spoiled for him. He still loved to be near horses, however, and he often drove Brian to Trot Inn.

Brian's sister Carla also liked to be in a saddle. Although not as old as Aunt Julia, she was too grown up to want to ride with Brian, or, of course, with a mere thirteen-year-old like Sunny.

This Sunday, when Carla came over after Sunday school and started being nice to Uncle Joe, Sunny suspected her of having designs on his car for transportation somewhere. Maybe to Trot Inn!

From the moment Carla's spike heels had tapped through the door, Sunny had not been able to take her eyes away from her. She was modish and pretty. Her hair was swept back from her face with a smart trimness that cried aloud "style." Sunny's hair was the despair of her life. It stayed in place about five minutes after combing. Would—*could* a hairdresser like Carla's make her equally devastating? The next second's thought reminded Sunny that Mother had settled it; the family budget could not stretch to beauty salons and horses, too. Of course there was no choice.

"So it really wouldn't be too much bother to drive me out to Trot Inn?" Carla asked.

Whew! Was Sunny glad Carla knew how to beguile her uncle! It was no trick at all to attach herself to the ride. Uncle Joe needed company on the return trip.

Carla even managed Aunt Julia's Sunday schedule. "You can get back before four easily. My friends will bring me home. They just didn't have time to come for me." Four o'clock was the Sunday dinner hour.

"We'll have to start soon," he admonished Carla.

Sunny doubted if Carla was a swift dresser, and her sheath dress, appropriate for church, would never do for riding. Sunny knew it was useless for her to change. Even if a horse were available on such a popular afternoon, there would not be time even for brief ring work. But she would be able to see Black Diamond again. That was joy enough.

After Carla left, Sunny asked, "Beau can go, too,

can't he?" She added, "Carla won't mind, will she?"

Aunt Julia gave a brief laugh. "Do you think that matters? But luckily she likes dogs—hairs and all."

Beau was Uncle Joe's dog and his inseparable companion, except when Aunt Julia was around.

"Beau," Uncle Joe had explained to Sunny, "is one perfect gentleman. I have told them if they want me to live here he must be welcome to the whole house. But he senses that he bothers Julia. Sometimes it hurts me the care he takes not to be in her way and how little she notices it."

Her attention called to it, Sunny watched the niceties of Beau's behavior. She wondered if many humans would be as forebearing as he was.

He gave up his front seat graciously to Carla, so Sunny slid in back with him. He rested his head on her knee and raised his big brown eyes to her gratefully. Beau's powers of expression were as wide as the scope of his All-American breed. Grace and bounding lightness came from the collie strain, with a lilt that shimmered in his long gold coat and white breast. Dependability came from the shepherd strain, which

gave him a smoother, broader forehead, in which snowy white shaped a little island. Rough, wiry hair on his top rear added a touch of Airedale pertness, which may have accounted, too, for his smallness.

Uncle Joe once commented to Sunny, "He's a hard size for a dog. He's too big for the little fellows and he's at a disadvantage with large dogs."

"He's got you, Uncle Joe. That's all he cares about."

Uncle Joe reached down to caress the head always so near him. "Maybe. But I think he'd enjoy more dog friends his own size to play with."

Sunny, looking down now at Beau beside her, wondered. He was always so good, so gentle and accepting. Never in the way of anybody.

Sunny, herself, on the ride out, was keeping very still. Carla was always a talker around men. She did not bother exerting herself when there were merely women around, and Sunny did not quite understand why Aunt Julia was more impressed with her than Uncle Joe was. Anyway he liked Carla enough to take her out to Trot Inn, for which, hurrah!

As they drove through the gateway, Carla saw her

friends at the mounting block. "Oh, let me out quick," she begged, opening the door even before Uncle Joe could stop the car. She flung back hastily, "Thanks for bringing me."

There was not an empty parking space in sight. "We can stop long enough to see Black Diamond, can't we?" cried Sunny in panic.

Her uncle smiled at her through the rearview mirror. "Don't worry. There's more room for cars around by the ring."

Sunny looked at her wristwatch. "It's almost an hour before dinnertime. Can't we stay out here half of it," she begged.

"Why not? You don't have to change when we get back."

Sunny tried not to appear impatient while Uncle Joe parked. His car had to be especially fitted for his artificial leg, but he was a very good driver. Only at the moment his every act about the car seemed an unnecessary delay in reaching the black horse. "Beau isn't allowed inside the stable so we'd better leave him here." He started rolling the windows up halfway.

"He'd probably stay in if I told him to, but with so many good smells it's kinder not to tempt him."

As they entered the stable, she said, "He was in a stall down that way."

"I thought they kept the rental horses on the other side in slip stalls."

"I guess they do. I wasn't over there. Brian did say there were boarder horses on this side, but I heard Mr. Donald tell Doug to put Diamond in a box stall."

"He probably needed one."

Sunny was trying not to get ahead of her uncle with his slow walk, but as she neared the stall she broke into a run.

"He's still here," she called back joyfully.

Black Diamond raised his head at the sound of her voice. "Oh, look! Uncle Joe, he knows me."

Her uncle did what Sunny would never have dared do without permission. He opened the stall door and motioned to her to follow him inside. The smell of fresh straw and clean horse was intoxicating.

Uncle Joe unbuckled the enveloping blanket and pulled it off, running his hands down the legs to Diamond's ankles. He stood back and gave him an appraising look.

"He's all right. They aren't swollen."

"Oh, isn't he wonderful?" Sunny could not refrain from giving him an impulsive hug.

Black Diamond flung back his head roughly, evading such familiarity. Ashamed of her presumption with such a proud creature, Sunny covered up by opening a bag she carried. She preferred to leave her purse in the drawer at home and stuff her pockets, but a dress appropriate for church had no place to carry carrots.

Diamond quickly discovered her treat and inclined her way again willingly. To pay him back for having shown her up, Sunny kept the carrot teasingly out of his reach. But only for a minute. He begged for it with such winning nudges of his long nose, grown now so gentle, she could not deprive him of it.

Sunny had learned something. Diamond liked carrots and he liked attention, but discriminating attention. He was not like a girl, pleased to be kissed just because some boy wanted to. His favors had to be won.

Mr. Donald noticed Uncle Joe and came over to

speak to them. Uncle Joe was replacing the blanket, but Mr. Donald said, "He doesn't really need it now and it's just as well to leave it off. We don't want to get him tender when he can't have a box stall all the time."

"He rates it," said Uncle Joe.

"Don't I know it!" said Mr. Donald feelingly. "He's a thousand times too good for regular rental work. But what can I do? I'm running a livery stable."

"I don't envy you—the way some of those kids ride."

"Not twice around here," replied Mr. Donald grimly. "I can see to it there's no racing the horses, no abuse. That's why, unless I know the rider, they go out in parties with somebody along I can trust. You'd be surprised how much I can depend on some of the boys like Brian and Douglas. And Kristy—she's another of our regulars—for the girls. But that doesn't save a horse like Diamond from too much of the daily grind. The time I had keeping him from them today! He has a little limp—not much, but some."

"Doug told Brian," Sunny spoke up with a beaming smile for the horse, "that if he'd been in a real race he would have broken records or something."

"Sure he would. But that gait didn't do Diamond's bones any good. A little rest today will help but he's so worn out he needs a full month of one rider—easy, easy going. And in the middle of my busiest season how can I pull that off?" Mr. Donald ended sadly.

Uncle Joe stroked his chin. "I've got an idea. I've a niece here with us old folks for a month. We want to keep her happy. Suppose I pay boarder box stall rates for Diamond and he can be her property for a month."

Sunny heard her uncle but she could not believe what she heard. She wanted to speak but she seemed unable to shape words, even get air into her lungs. She was floundering in excitement. It was too wonderful. She could not be hearing right.

Mr. Donald's face brightened. "Do you mean it? Will she be willing to ride him gently?"

Uncle Joe answered, "I've seen Sunny ride in the East. I know Diamond has a sensitive mouth and resents a tight rein. She's the rider for him. She has good hands, gentle but she keeps control."

"Oh, Uncle Joe, are you really talking about me?" Sunny gasped out. Could he possibly mean her, Sara

Lu Saunders, mostly known as Sunny?

"I sure am. I take it you'd like this arrangement."

"Like it! Oh, I'd be the happiest girl in the world!"

"I wonder if you understand entirely." Mr. Donald waited until he had her attention before going on. "If we are really to get Diamond back in shape he ought to be ridden mostly alone. Anyway at first. Even if I give him a few days' rest before you start."

"I don't mind not going in a group. Just let me walk him around in the ring. Anything to be on him!"

Uncle Joe put in, "She's safe enough alone in the pasture, isn't she?"

"Perfectly. Diamond only throws off riders who get too bossy with him. He has bumped off nearly every man on the place. They like to get him all excited—then get smart with him. He won't stand for it and he's an expert at neatly dumping them. Not mean about it. Just very effective."

Uncle Joe laughed. "The faces I've seen on some men walking in! But I've been around enough to know I'm safe trusting Sunny on him. The problem is going to be transportation on weekdays. But I think I can work it in before I go to the office and on noon hours. If necessary I'll take time off. I don't have a niece visiting me often and luckily there are few rush projects on right now."

"We'll help all we can. There're always cars going back and forth, anyway as far as a bus."

Sunny kept stealing glances away from the speakers, much as she wanted to follow what they were saying, but she had to look at Black Diamond to be sure he was real. Hers! Hers for a whole month! Had any other girl in the world ever been this lucky?

As the two men walked toward the tack room, Sunny slipped back to the horse's stall. She had a last carrot for him. Luckily any number of carrots were good for a horse. How was she ever going to buy enough? She'd find out what she ate that cost the most and give that up. Then surely Aunt Julia would approve of buying more carrots.

As Diamond greedily crunched her last one, she whispered to him, "Oh, I'll be so good to you. And I won't make you mad trying to hug you. I'll just hug you inside me."

3

The First Ride

Monday started as a dull day. The novelty of visiting a new place was wearing off. Even the joy of Black Diamond was slowing down. Thinking about him made Sunny want to be in the saddle, and he was to rest today.

She wanted to talk about him to friends, but who was there she could even telephone? Brian had a summer job at a supermarket. Kristy, another neighbor she had seen a bit of, was taking her music lesson and afterward going to see her grandmother.

Sunny hated letter writing. At home Mother would keep at her until she did it, but around here no one pushed disagreeable duties on a guest. She limited her writing to her family and to her close friend Ruth, whose long letters she had answered with brief lines. But then, Ruth liked to write letters.

She could not even help Aunt Julia with the wash, for there was no long line to fill with wet laundry like the one at home. Aunt Julia had an automatic dryer. The cleaning woman was coming tomorrow, so dusting was wasted energy. And Aunt Julia was more bothered than helped by having anyone around while she cooked.

Sunny finished the breakfast dishes and went up to her room, Beau at her heels. Ordinarily he stayed in Uncle Joe's room in his absence, but lately, if he could not be with Sunny, he sought her room. Before she made her bed, Sunny sat down to pet him. Then she remembered.

There was something she could do. She had promised Uncle Joe to play ball with Beau.

"Since they got that leash law and we have to keep him in so much he doesn't get enough exercise," Uncle Joe had worried.

And here when her uncle was doing so much for her, giving her a dream horse all her own for a month, she had almost forgotten her promise.

She had to do her room first, so she went after it

with a vim that restored order in no time. When there was a point in getting it done, she pitched in without effort.

Beau liked a hard rubber ball, and Uncle Joe had a plentiful supply on hand. The first ball she tossed, the dog missed. Sunny looked surprised, and Beau very ashamed. Then she remembered.

"Dogs," Uncle Joe had told her, "have very poor sight but marvelous hearing. I've discovered Beau locates the ball with his ears, not his eyes. An airplane buzzing overhead will get him off. He misses his catch often if the hose is running with its whirring sound."

Hoses were always running on lawns in Denver. Newcomers to town were delighted at the green, green grass; then when they found what work watering it involved, they were less enthusiastic. Without the watering, lawns were not simply less green, as in Illinois, but here they dried up and disappeared.

Mere Odette had a yard man, and he had left a hose running in the backyard while he made a round of neighborhood lawns, changing the positions of nozzles. Sunny knew it would not matter if she turned off the water long enough for a game with Beau.

He was watching the ball in her hands, his plume tail in violent motion. She took careful aim, so she could throw it high yet still have it come down within the rather small backyard. Beau's excitement grew.

Up, up, up went that thrilling ball, then down, down, and up, up, up he went to meet it, with paws a full yard off the ground as he made a perfect catch. Proudly he returned.

"Good work!" Sunny praised him warmly. "Give it here and I'll throw it again."

Beau pulled back, torn with conflicting emotions. He had put all his heart into that leap and he had got the ball. Now it was his ball. His! Yet this girl was reaching for it. His ball! Still, if he let her have it she would throw it up in the air again. He could leap again to catch it. Finally he reluctantly dropped it at her feet; the next moment he was all eagerness for the chase.

The game could have gone on for the rest of the day, to Beau's satisfaction, but the yard man returned. Sunny appeased him by promising to water the missed spots later herself. He showed her where to do it.

"That's my last. I let it run there a good half hour."

After he had gone, Sunny soon found herself tired of tossing balls. "You've had enough exercise," she told Beau. "You don't want Uncle Joe to find you all tired out."

His lively dark eyes showed him far from tired, so she added, "We'd better do this watering before we forget it."

She turned the hose on again and walked out to the front yard, trailed by Beau, ball in mouth.

The hoses were off in front, so while she waited for the back one to do its job, she bounced the ball hard on the paved walk. It came down at a new angle that nearly somersaulted Beau catching it, but he was ready for the new approach with the next bounce and caught that expertly.

By noon, his interest in catches each so alike was flagging some, and Sunny's was completely.

"The yard's soaked enough," she told Beau, "and it's time for lunch."

Beau, like a sensible dog, was not interested in food in the middle of the day, but Sunny was boss. He helped

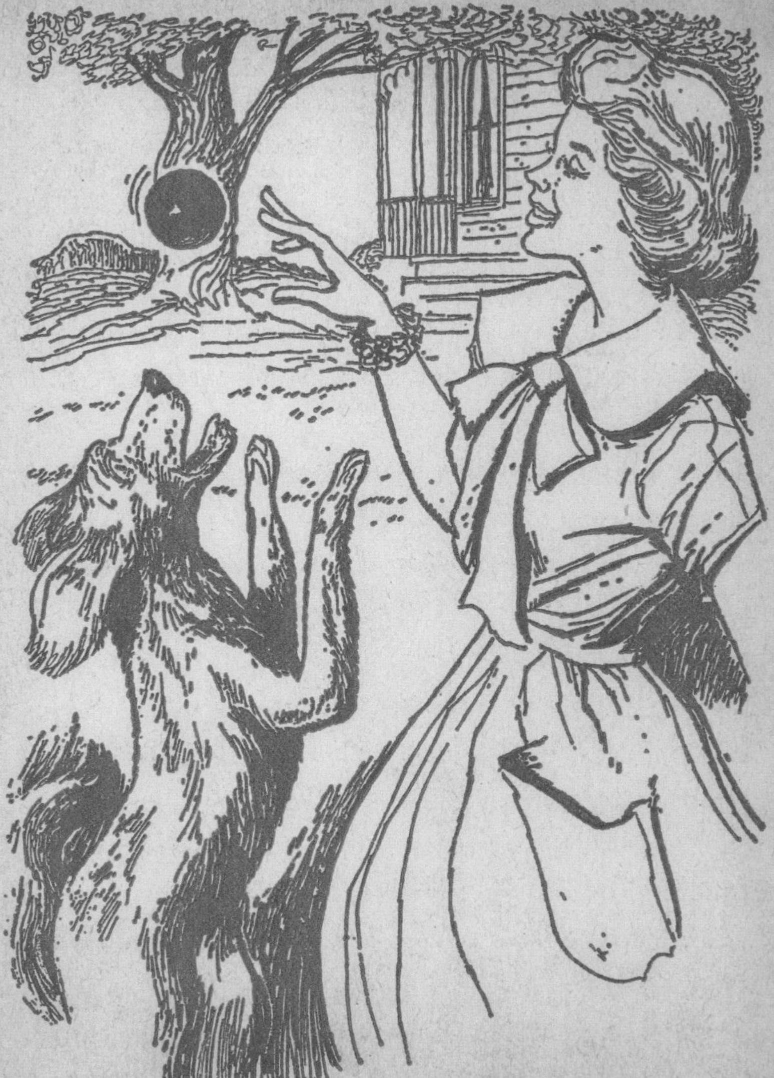

her turn off the hose and entered the house with her, separating at the door. He went to her room, while Sunny found *Mere* Odette and Aunt Julia in the living room, engaged in a somewhat heated discussion. Usually they got along pleasantly for all their different tastes.

This afternoon, Aunt Julia planned to attend a meeting of a French society and insisted *Mere* Odette go along. "You know you always like everything French and this society has nice members."

Mere Odette's sweet little face had a scowl new to Sunny. "And they think their talk is such wonderful French and they're just showing off. I can't understand a word they say. They expect me to because I was in Paris so long."

"Well, you were. You know you were. And they have some of the best society people in town for members."

"Is that why you stand for all that French they want to jabber?"

Sunny could not resist putting in, "But, Grandmother, you know you've told me how many of your things you like because they're French."

Mere Odette wheeled on her in a fury. "You impudent child! Keep still."

Surprised, Sunny flung back, "But it's true."

Mere Odette glared at her in speechless rage. All at once Sunny grasped that the temper came from knowing Aunt Julia was really in the right, and what she had said made it worse.

Aunt Julia waved a shushing hand at her, then she herself made *Mere* Odette even angrier. "Oh, all right. If you won't go I'll tell them you're sick. So don't dare let them see you looking perfectly well when they call for me. I'll get lunch right away."

It was not a pleasant meal. Neither of the grownups spoke, and Sunny kept still, too, envying Beau his chance to sneak up to her room and stay there.

After they finished eating, *Mere* Odette stalked off. Sunny offered, "Let me do the dishes alone, Aunt Julia. You'll have more time to dress. I know now where everything goes."

"If you will," Aunt Julia consented gratefully. "I don't know why those ladies have to want Mother and won't like it when she stays home."

"Maybe," Sunny ventured, "they can't find enough people who like French things. I don't."

Aunt Julia broke into a peal of rare laughter, but she made no reply.

Mere Odette stayed in her room with a closed door.

"Better not try to go in," Aunt Julia advised before leaving. "I'm sorry I got her so upset."

Beau joined Sunny in the big, dreary living room, but he was not much company. Content with his morning's fun, he slept with a dog's utter relaxation. He was restful to look at but not very entertaining. Sunny tried a book, but lost interest after the first page. The pictures in the magazines were dull. She could not find a deck of cards for solitaire. Time dragged slower and slower.

Beau barked for the mailman and Sunny rushed to see if there was anything in the slot for her. Hurray! Another letter from Ruth.

Sunny's eyes raced down the page. Bits of news of many friends, none very exciting. Then Sunny's gaze slowed. She read more and more carefully.

I don't know. I may give up riding. Sunny, I'm doing worse and worse with you gone. Yesterday I fell off Torchy. He dumped me so neatly and so scornfully when I made him mad not letting him do what he wanted to.

Sunny was in despair. Why, oh, why had Colonel Dwyer let her go out on Torchy? The worst horse in the world for Ruth, a girl scared of horses to start with! Mr. Donald and her uncle had been raving at the way rental riders mistreated horses. They should know Torchy. He shared their disapproval of a lot of his riders, but he had learned how to handle them. He could give a smooth, lovely ride when he felt like it, but if he didn't, he could punish their seats. The Colonel had probably thought Ruth, with her power of balance, her good knee grips, could handle any gait, and make Torchy behave. The horse had probably felt the same, only he did not want to behave, and then he may have sensed her inner fear. Anyway he'd given her the unexpected stop, the jolt to slide her off. He was not really mean. None of his riders got hurt, but many were humiliated. And now Ruth!

Oh, dear, oh, dear! It was queer how a girl could worship horses as Ruth did and still be so afraid of them. Somehow not of them but of her own riding ability. Sunny had puzzled over it. Ruth was such a grand friend, they were so close, yet she could never pour into her the confidence she needed. Now to have this happen!

Sunny forgot she hated letter writing and poured out her protests to Ruth. She must not give up riding, not even until Sunny's return. Every day lost, feeling as she did, built up her fear. Sunny hesitated. Should she advise her to ride Torchy? In most cases, yes, after a tumble. But Torchy was certainly no horse for Ruth.

If only she could talk to the Colonel, the owner of the riding academy, Timber Trail Farm! He was always so understanding—what had happened to make him act so? Still he had never seemed to quite understand Ruth's case. She was not a dumbbell rider like most scaries, and few had been close enough to Ruth to glimpse the depth of her inner fear. Sunny tried to tell her all riders were afraid sometimes. Maybe part of the thrill in riding was the satisfaction of overcoming it. But she had not convinced Ruth, who was certain no one else was the baby she was. Yet how she loved horses! And that rascal Torchy had had to shake her confidence still more!

Sunny was torn with longing to be with her. She filled another page with pleadings for her to ride, ride, ride. She listed all the horses that would be better than Torchy. Yes, Ruth had better stay off Torchy.

At four the telephone rang. Uncle Joe said he had talked with Mr. Donald who was certain a little ring work would not hurt Black Diamond. Did Sunny want him to take her out?

Did she! "How soon can you come for me?" she begged. "I can be ready in two minutes. Beau goes, too, doesn't he? I know he wants to get out of this house as much as I do."

"Why? Anything wrong up there?"

"Oh, not much. I'll tell you later. Hurry now, won't you, please? I just can't wait to see Diamond."

"Ho-ho! So that's the trouble, is it?" replied a relieved Uncle Joe.

What had he been afraid was wrong? Sunny did not have time to puzzle over it now. She must get into the right clothes. Beau approved of what she was putting on. He was eager to go, too. He kept trying to press a long beseeching nose against her knee.

"Beau, how can I dress with you there? Don't worry, I'm sure you can go."

Mere Odette heard her and came in to find what was up. She lost interest when she learned it was horseback riding.

Sunny urged, "Why don't you come out for the ride? I do want you to see Black Diamond. We won't be away long."

Mere Odette wavered, then objected, "No. No, it will be windy."

The wind had been coming up. It could get very unpleasant out at Trot Inn. "Maybe another time," Sunny agreed.

"You say you'll be home soon?"

Sunny knew how *Mere* Odette hated to be alone in the house. "Very. Aunt Julia should be back even sooner. She said the meeting was over at four thirty."

"She'll want to tell me all about it and I don't want to hear. I'm going back to my room." She marched off.

Sunny grabbed up a sweater and raced for the stairs. Didn't she hear Uncle Joe downstairs? Beau did not need to be staying so close to her. Uncle Joe rarely left him behind. Of course he did not this afternoon. The three of them lost no time settling into the front seat of the green convertible.

Once they were well started, Uncle Joe asked, "Now what was the trouble you were talking about?"

Sunny had wanted to discuss Ruth's letter with him. Instead she had to try to explain the disagreement between his mother and his sister. She did not see any point to most of it, but she could repeat what had been said. Uncle Joe looked more and more troubled.

"Is that society so important?" Sunny finally asked.

Uncle Joe turned his eyes from the street to meet hers briefly. "It's not important at all. What matters is Julia. Mother, as she gets older, is growing more and more demanding. Julia always gives in to her. She has too little life of her own and since she is so pleased at being asked to join this society it is wrong of Mother to act this way. If I tell her so it will just make her worse. I don't know what to do."

Sunny knew it was not her place to offer advice so she kept still. Finally he said with a sigh, "I guess just leave them alone and let it blow over." Then to Sunny's satisfaction he turned to the all important subject. "Mr. Donald says Diamond is acting so much peppier today he thinks a little ring work would do him good."

"You mean more than just walking him?"

"If he isn't limping."

"Oh, how I hope he won't be!"

Sunny felt as if, if the car's engine stopped, her own throbbing eagerness would keep them speeding toward the stables. Soon she would be actually on Black Diamond's back. Oh, it took a long time getting out to Trot Inn!

"I didn't see Mother around," remarked Uncle Joe. "Where was she?"

"Up in her room with the door shut."

"What a nice way to spoil all of Julia's pleasure in

that French meeting of hers!"

"*Mere* Odette is usually so sweet."

Uncle Joe's lips were grim. "When she's having her own way. If she were a horse I could make her see how foolish she's acting—that is, I could once."

"*Mere* Odette a horse!" Sunny's laughter rang out. "Why she doesn't even like horses. Oh, Uncle Joe, you are funny."

"Not funny. Foolish. Of course giving in to her has been the easiest way. But I should have seen it was Julia who has to pay."

Sunny's merriment subsided at his severe tone. She wondered in astonishment if she needed to apologize for laughing. Then she forgot everything but a black horse. They were turning into the gateway.

In a moment Rod led out Diamond, already saddled, his coat shining from recent brushing, his head held high. Her horse! Rod lightly tapped his front legs and Diamond stretched out low enough for Sunny to mount from the ground, foot in stirrup. He stayed motionless while she gathered up the reins.

"The stirrups need to be a little shorter," she said.

Rod quickly adjusted the buckles, and she was ready to start.

The extra attentions given Diamond excited him. Sensitive always to his rider's feelings, he absorbed Sunny's feeling of this being a great event. Lifting each foot high, Diamond moved toward the ring as if at the head of a parade passing lines of spectators.

Each step beat into Sunny's heart. Her horse! Hers! They went evenly around the ring, deserted now in Monday calm.

There was not a trace of a limp. Uncle Joe, Beau at his side, watched her from the ring's edge. "Take him into a trot."

Sunny tightened her hold on the reins in unison with a pressure of her legs and thighs. First a slow trot, then she urged a swifter pace, and the even beat of his hoofs had the rhythm of music from the *Tales of Hoffman.*

Twice around, then again. Now a controlled walk for a rest. Next she swung him toward the rail for the proper lead and took him into a canter. Briefly she let him go faster, faster, sensing his longing to show her exactly what he could do.

But she slowed him down and changed to a trot again. Once around and again a walk, which she kept up till the tenseness left his muscles. After all, according to first plans he was not supposed to have been ridden today. She must not ride him too long. There would be tomorrow and tomorrow. She wheeled him toward the gate of the ring.

Mr. Donald materialized from somewhere. "You'll do. It was a good bargain for Diamond your uncle made with me. Now I know how very good."

Oh, if she had not come through, how Sunny would have hated herself!

As he took the horse from her at the stable door, Mr. Donald said, "I'd try riding in the pasture next time. You'll both enjoy it more."

"Thank you. I'd love to." But she wanted to tell him he was crazy thinking anybody could ever enjoy anything more than she had her ride today. Sunny wondered if she'd ever understand the way adults thought.

"I'll see she gets out tomorrow sometime," Uncle Joe promised Mr. Donald.

4   *"Horses Are Tops!"*

Driving back, Sunny was in a state of ecstatic happiness. Beau felt it and sneaked his long nose up to her chin for a loving lick of endorsement. Beau did think it a pity most humans disliked dogs' best way of expressing themselves, but he knew Sunny understood tongue language.

However, ordinarily, she remembered to discourage it or he'd be doing it to the wrong people. Right now she just had to respond to each lick with a quick, loving squeeze. Uncle Joe was looking happy, too.

They breezed gaily into the house, talking horse, the quarrel forgotten, but they were at once reminded of it. Aunt Julia's eyes were pink-rimmed, and *Mere* Odette was still in her room.

"Dinner's ready any time," said Aunt Julia. "I know you two are hungry so why don't we sit right down?

Sunny, will you go up and get your grandmother?"

Mere Odette answered Sunny's knock by darting across the room and flinging open the door. She was freshly dressed for dinner and greeted Sunny with smiling fondness.

"My dear, I see from your face the ride was a success."

"Oh, yes! I must tell you all about it. But Aunt Julia says we are to come right down to dinner."

"I'm sure," said *Mere* Odette in honeyed tones, "she did not mean for you not to change."

"She said I need not bother today. We're all so hungry."

Mere Odette, disapproval in every line of her tiny body, pointed to the pants. "I am sure, my dear, you did not understand her. Go dress at once."

Sunny bit back her answer. Quicker to change than to argue. Within minutes she was taking the stairs down, two at a time.

"Dinner is getting very cold," Aunt Julia told her, "but I understand it is not your fault."

Mere Odette patted her arm. "You were a good,

obedient child," she praised her in a sugared voice.

Before Sunny could grow more uncomfortable, Uncle Joe rescued her. "Let's get to the table. Sunny wants to tell you about her ride. She's a true horseman!"

"Isn't it a horsewoman?" suggested Aunt Julia. "Anyway, Sunny, I'm delighted you are so good at it. We must see you get in a lot of riding."

Sunny listened in a daze. Here she had thought Aunt Julia did not like animals. "Won't you come out to see Diamond? I know you'll love him."

Mere Odette interrupted, "Joe, will you pass me some bread, please? If everybody hasn't been too interested in horses to remember to put it on."

"Here we are, Mother. With slices cut in half exactly as you like them."

His mother accepted them ungraciously. "Wholewheat bread again! White is so to be preferred."

Aunt Julia made no response, though Friday Sunny had heard *Mere* Odette especially asking for wholewheat bread. Uncle Joe turned to his sister and urged, "I wish you would take Sunny out tomorrow. I know you avoid using your car all you can but there's little traffic during the day, and I think it would do you good to be away from the house more," he ended bluntly.

His mother blinked at him in astonishment, while his sister gave him a smile. "Maybe you're right."

Sunny encouraged her. "You won't have long to wait. I'm to ride less than an hour my first time in the pasture."

"I won't mind waiting in the least," Aunt Julia agreed.

This was too much for *Mere* Odette. She forgot she was not speaking to her daughter. "Julia! Tomorrow is the day you bake bread. You can't leave that."

Aunt Julia's spunk was up. "Can't I? You'll be surprised how easily I manage." She turned to Sunny. "Don't worry. You won't be hurried at all."

Mere Odette pushed back her chair and gathered herself together. "I think I had better go to my room," she stated severely and waited. No one was in a mood to apologize or urge her to stay.

Sunny ventured, "Can I help you carry anything

up—or—or do anything else?"

This was nothing like the attentions *Mere* Odette had been bidding for. She caught her breath several times as if about to speak, then her gaze left the adults to focus on Sunny. "You are kind. Our family seems to be acting very strangely. Yes, I must go to my room and you may come up and read to me."

Sunny groaned inwardly. So this was what she had let herself in for! She was not a good reader and hated to do it. "I was going to do all the dishes for Aunt Julia. I didn't help at all setting table."

"I'm certain my daughter can manage without your services," said *Mere* Odette stiffly. "You come upstairs with me."

"Go on, Sunny," added Uncle Joe. "Diamond'll make it up to you tomorrow."

The lead left Sunny's feet. She could read dull pages all night if that led to riding her horse.

But it was not all night. *Mere* Odette was as bored as Sunny with the book she had selected. She fell asleep delightfully soon and was soon snoring. Sunny turned out the reading light and put on the night one, and left. *Mere* Odette thought snoring was vulgar. Nobody had ever told her she did it herself.

Downstairs Sunny found Aunt Julia looking much happier. Uncle Joe had known the right things to say. Now if only she would still want to drive out to Trot Inn! Sunny wondered if it would be wiser to wait till morning before she said anything.

Her worry was wasted. Aunt Julia was taking it for granted she was going.

"I was wondering about Beau. Joe tells me he had a wonderful time today and that Mr. Donald said it would be all right for him to go to the pasture with you."

"Wouldn't you mind him in your car?" asked Sunny.

"Why? He is really a very well-behaved dog. I'm certain he'll stay quiet in the back seat."

"Oh, he will!" Sunny ejaculated happily. So, after all, Beau's earnest efforts not to bother Aunt Julia had been appreciated and were to be rewarded.

Mere Odette had breakfast in bed. Sunny was glad to give service carrying trays, and no one was too worried about her "headache."

Uncle Joe was still unrelenting. He said crossly, "If she wants to enjoy having one let her go ahead with it, but don't let it interfere with any of your plans."

"Sunny will get her ride," her aunt promised.

"Take care of yourself, too. Remember it's time right now to stop her growing demands on you."

It had been settled to go out to Trot Inn in the morning, while it was still cool.

"How about your bread? You haven't got it started," Sunny reminded Aunt Julia as she rushed preparations to be off.

Her brother came back from the door to pat her on the back. "Go to it."

"We'll just stack the dishes. They can wait. It's time I'm seeing that black horse."

Sunny wondered what her uncle could have told her to arouse this lively interest in Diamond. They talked about nothing else on the way out, so Sunny thoroughly enjoyed the ride. It was a perfect day to be out, sunny but not too hot. She watched Aunt Julia anxiously as Rod brought out Diamond. Would her aunt think him as wonderful as she did?

Diamond knew he was being inspected and liked it, just as he had enjoyed the preliminary grooming. The horse needed rest, but the space in a box stall was limited, even though it was an improvement on a slip stall. Diamond was ready for variety. He made mounting him as exciting as he possibly could.

"Are you sure you can handle him?" Aunt Julia grew alarmed. "Should you take him out alone?"

"She'll be all right," Rod said positively.

As if in denial, Diamond, once Rod's detaining hold on his reins was gone, started off in a prancing dance, but Sunny at once realized how easily she was keeping her seat. He was certainly an artist at showing off. To reassure her aunt, Sunny took Diamond circling around the deserted parking space, demonstrating that *she* was in control, not the horse, so Aunt Julia relaxed.

Beau was having a treat exploring smells. Pal, the black ranch dog, had finally been made to understand that he must not interfere with visiting dogs. He did not approve of Beau's presence—his manner was anything but friendly—but he stayed in the background. Beau tried to pretend he did not see him.

Rod asked Sunny, "Want me to open the gate for you? Or do you want to see how Diamond can help?"

"Oh, please, let me open it myself."

"Try the one over there." He pointed to a lane on the side of the stables where Sunny had not been. "Mr. Donald put in a wooden gate to make it easier for riders. You come out in the same pasture."

Waving good-bye to Aunt Julia and whistling for Beau to come with her, Sunny wheeled Diamond and trotted off. She watched how cautiously Beau kept his distance from them. The dog had obviously been impressed the day before at her riding that great black horse. Then he had stayed with Uncle Joe. Now he was to adventure out with her.

Mr. Donald had cautioned her, "Just don't let him go straying off or let him get too close to Diamond. Keep an eye on him."

He had been busy investigating smells as she was starting. Now he was following behind, but wisely not too close. It was going to be easy having him along.

Sunny had never opened a gate before. She was glad

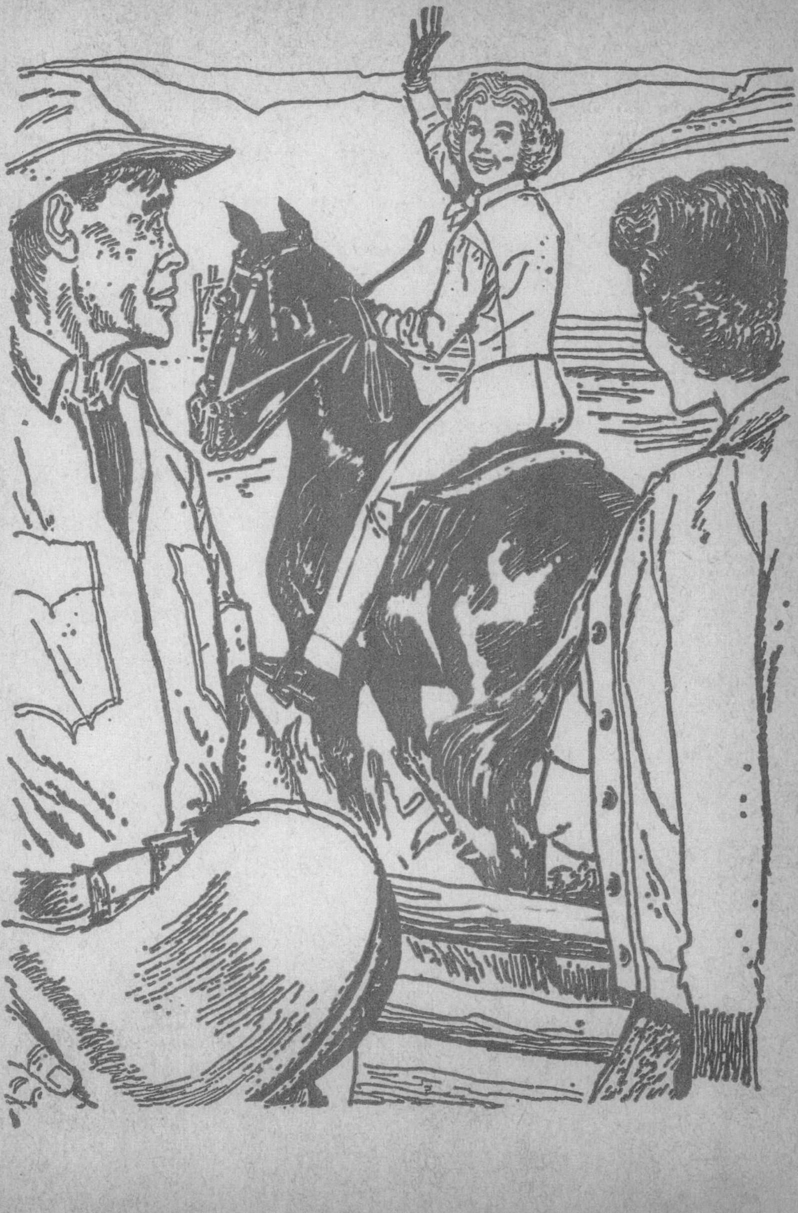

that for her first experience she was not going to tackle one with loose wires like the one she had helped Brian open on foot. Here the slatted frame swung on hinges from a firm post. Wire loops over another post held it shut. To make it easy for riders, the only fastening was at the top. Why, it was no trick at all to guide Diamond close, reach over, and release it.

The gate gave an unexpected swing in her direction, almost hitting Diamond before she pushed out her stirrup and kicked it in the other direction. She could imagine how some horses would have reacted. Diamond stood helpfully still, then as they moved through, his long nose reached around for a shove to keep it well away from them. She had been holding out a guarding hand but it was scarcely needed.

Once through, she gave Diamond an approving pat. "Nice work, fellow." She reined him around to close it. That was easier, as she had only to push it shut and quickly slip the retaining loop over the post. With a clear road ahead, she took Diamond into a pleased trot.

All at once she remembered Beau. He had been

busy around the gate with so many smells to investigate, but now where was he? She should not have forgotten him.

The lane ahead was straight for some distance. She could see him easily if he were there. He was not coming along behind. He was not in the open field to one side. She looked for him in the corral on the other side. No dog. Alarmed, she stopped Diamond and wheeled him around. What had happened to Beau?

Then she saw him. Way back, behind the gate, a forlorn dog was sitting, gazing woefully after her. She had deliberately left him behind. On either side of the riders' gate were barbed-wire fences, with plenty of open spaces he could have slipped through. But to a poor little city hick, a closed door meant you were barred out.

Sunny went back and with Diamond's help solemnly opened the gate. Beau, with reviving happiness, bounded through, his plumed tail waving. The rest of the ride he took care to be very near her when they came to gates.

Sunny was familiar with cottonwood trees, but

today she came to know them in a new way. They had no shapely, groomed comeliness. Their beauty belonged not to cultivated gardens but to untended nature. They patterned the sun in loveliness on the grassy sands of the creek bottoms. They pulled peace about her.

Cottonwoods made wonderful goal posts for a riding game, as she wove great figure eights around them. Vegetation had padded enough body into the sand for perfect track work. Diamond's canter was fluid gliding joy in motion. If only Ruth were here!

This was the kind of riding Ruth needed. Surely, if she had started here, her confidence would have built up faster than any fear could have.

She and Ruth were alike in so many ways. They were both tall, slender, with good enough figures so clothes did not flop too badly on them, but neither had showy good looks, none of the rose-petal skin or magic smiles of book heroines. They both had undistinguished hair. Ruth's would not even shape into lustrous style with combing and brushing as Sunny's would. But then, Sunny's stayed that way less than twenty minutes.

Both were well liked and made friends easily, but no one ever seemed to think about nominating them for any top office. The job that nobody else wanted usually came their way. They were among the "ins," not the "outs," but it would be fun sometime to be a little outstanding.

Sunny could have lingered happily in the pasture for hours, but her watch told her that her time was almost gone. In reward for turning stableward, she discovered that Diamond's trot was even better on the harder path of the lane. After a bit she slowed him reluctantly to a walk. He was not in the least overheated so a fairly brief one sufficed.

Aunt Julia was waiting at the gate. "Oh, Auntie, was I gone too long? Did you get tired waiting?"

"Not a bit. It's such a lovely day I wished I'd told you I was going for a walk down there. But I didn't want you to come back and find me gone. I'll do it next time."

Sunny's face lighted. "You mean you don't mind there being a next time?"

"I'll bring you any time your uncle can't."

Mr. Donald joined them at the stable door. He looked approvingly at Diamond, munching his last carrot. "He's coming up already, isn't he? I can see you had a good ride. By Saturday Diamond should be ready for a long ride. Why don't you join the group going out?"

Aunt Julia put in, "I hope she can. She needs to be with more young people."

Mr. Donald pointed to Sunny's face, glowing with pleasure. "Well, she doesn't seem to be suffering too much."

"Oh, Mr. Donald, I didn't know riding a horse alone would be so different. You're so much closer to him."

He nodded. "That's true." Then he added, "But do both."

The moment she was in the house, Sunny reached for the mail slot. No new letter from Ruth.

That evening, Brian stopped by on the way home from his job. He thought she was mistaken about riding alone. "Horses pep each other up. Try riding Diamond with us and you'll see."

"Wednesday, Thursday, Friday," Sunny counted days on her fingers. "Three more that I keep rides short. Mr. Donald thinks he'll be ready by Saturday."

"I hope I get to ride Starlight," Brian said. "She's one of Midnight's colts and her owner isn't riding her enough. Mr. Donald trusts me and lets me ride her so she can get more exercise. The trouble is the crowd is set to do the big ditch circle and then we have to go by a house with a mean dog. Maybe I couldn't handle Starlight around him."

"Tomorrow Aunt Julia is going to leave me out there all afternoon while she does errands. Do you think I can see Starlight?"

"Ask Rod to show you the roan mare. He will. He'll let you groom Diamond, too, if you want to."

"Who wouldn't? Oh, Brian, isn't it bliss just to be around horses?"

"You girls go nuts," Brian scoffed.

"But you do like to groom your horse, don't you?" Sunny pressed him. "You don't call that work."

"Oh, sure," Brian had to admit sheepishly. "Yeah, you win, Sunny. Horses are tops."

5   *Four-Legged Bully*

When Sunny brought out her riding clothes, Beau remembered his fun of the day before and followed her with frantic pleading. He tried to tell her with his paw how interested he was, but that interfered with her dressing and plainly did not please her. He sat back, his great beseeching eyes fastened on her every move.

"Oh, Beau! Stop worrying. You're going."

Her tone, even more than her words, reassured him, but Beau wanted to be certain. He could not relax until the car door was opened and he leaped in, sitting carefully on the cover spread for him and his doggy hairs.

He was happier still when they opened the back window. News was no longer blurred. He could poke out his nose and take in the gossip that smells spelled out for him. Here were proper dog newspapers. Sunny wished they included Illinois papers. Maybe those would tell if Ruth was riding. Probably not.

Aunt Julia let them out at the gateway at one o'clock. "I'll make it back about five. Be a good girl and don't get in their way. I'm not worrying about time dragging for you."

"You don't need to worry about anything," Sunny assured her.

Her delight increased when she saw Mr. Donald saddling his latest colt, and he said she could come with him.

"I have to go to a neighbor's down the road but you won't have any trouble with Diamond and cars. Just watch Beau when one's coming. There aren't many at this hour."

As they rode out of the gate, he commented, "I'm glad to have Diamond along. A colt pays attention to an older horse. Daylight may get sense someday but she sure can do fool things now."

"Has she been outside the ranch much?"

Mr. Donald shook his head. "That's why I'm taking

her now. She needs to learn. The longer I keep her off the road, the harder it will be later. Fortunately she likes Pal or I'd shut the dogs up."

At first Beau clung close behind, but Pal, while never going far from the riders, found much here and there that Beau was certain must be of great interest. He made tentative advances to join Pal and found him not unfriendly. Pal was unhappy when newcomers invaded his home quarters, but reinforcements were welcome in possibly hostile territory. Sunny was pleased to see the dogs become friends.

"With two dogs of our own along," Mr. Donald remarked, "fewer strange ones run out at us. The less there is to upset Daylight the better."

The young horse seemed to Sunny to behave very well. The filly wanted to fuss with her bit, but her rider stopped that every time she started and soon she gave up, accepting its guidance. Diamond showed scorn at any offbeat movement of hers in a way plain to a horse if not to humans. She quickly stopped sudden dancing steps to the side and moved in line with his leadership.

"See—he's good for her." Mr. Donald broke a silence that somehow went with the ride.

Sunny smiled down at her horse. "He seems to know she needs training and he's trying to be extra steady around her."

"He knows what we expect of him around colts all right. I guess he himself believes they need disciplining. As far as our ranch horses have a leader, he's it."

Sunny would have liked to hear more about this leadership, but Mr. Donald lapsed again into silence, as if words were not needed around four-footed friends who never used them.

A car appeared and they drew to the side of the graveled road to let it pass, watching that the dogs stayed out of its way. As they came to the next house, Mr. Donald again broke the silence. "They have a mean dog there."

"Is it the one Brian is afraid to ride near?"

He nodded. "I think today he'll see Pal has another dog with him and stay back."

Apparently the dog did count dog noses. Anyway they saw no sign of him.

Half a mile beyond, Mr. Donald turned into a driveway. "I shouldn't be here long but it's hard waiting with horses. Why don't you start back slowly and I'll catch up with you."

"All right."

Diamond approved of starting home and backed up the suggestion with eager obedience. Daylight went into a tirade of prancing protest at being left behind, and her rider had to deal with her severely. Sunny left her still wheeling in circles. Beau followed not far behind Diamond, no longer interested in side explorations without Pal.

The young horse's lively energy had been pushing old Diamond's gaits, and now he subsided into a slower and slower walk. Sunny relaxed in the saddle, enjoying a summer day away from city streets.

Abruptly Diamond tensed under her. He had heard something she missed. Ahead was the house with the mean dog, and this time there was only one enemy. The bully could go for this party.

Beau saw him. He had his master's niece to protect. He would not run away from his responsibility. He came to stand between them, but he knew as well as Sunny that he was no fighter. He had no chance with the scarred veteran coming at him, snarling viciously. Fear shook both Beau and Sunny.

Diamond felt it and acted. He moved so that Beau was almost under him, but his hoofs did not touch him. The horse's teeth were bared. His heels were ready for a swift kick. Any dog approaching was in for stern measures, and the bully knew it. He slunk away in craven terror, looking back in grateful relief that he was not being followed.

Then, and then only, Diamond backed away from the dog he had been protecting. Sunny urged him into a desperate gallop, back to Mr. Donald, calling wildly, "Beau! Beau! Come on. Stay with us."

She wasted breath. Beau had no intention of being left behind. He raced with them, as close to Diamond as he dared.

They reached the farmhouse, with Sunny still disheveled. Mr. Donald rushed out to meet them, very alarmed. "What happened?"

Sunny was too terrified for coherent speech at first,

but soon she gave a full account, toning down nothing.

"You mean," Mr. Donald interrupted, "Diamond let Beau between his hoofs? Why, he never lets a dog anywhere near him. He gets along with them all right but he's afraid of tripping on them, and they must stay away from his feet."

"He had to protect Beau," Sunny cried. "Don't you see? That awful dog was about to chew him up."

"I've got to believe you." He still looked dubious. "Well, we'll have Pal along to help going home. We'd better get started. Now slow down." He looked with disapproval at Diamond's still-heaving sides. Fortunately the horse had not given in enough to the girl's fright to get himself in too much of a sweat reaching Mr. Donald.

As they again approached the house, the dog was out in front. Their own two dogs were well in the rear. The bully saw Diamond first. He did not stop for a second look at anything. Tail down he ran. No one could doubt what sent him slinking back into his yard, on to the shelter behind.

Mr. Donald nodded to Sunny. "You win. Diamond

settled that dog all right. I'd say you were perfectly safe to ride by that house any day."

"Would it be all right for Brian to take Starlight along—if Diamond goes?" She pressed this advantage eagerly.

He laughed. "Well, now that needs thinking about. Maybe."

Anyway the "maybe" was nearer "yes" than it had been before. Sunny had an idea Brian would ride Starlight.

As she and Mr. Donald rode through the gateway, Pal scooted ahead and went into the house yard. Beau started to follow, but was stopped by an unfriendly growl. Beau, trying to look as if nothing had happened, returned to the horses and waited around the stable door. Pal's friendship plainly ended at Trot Inn grounds.

It seemed to her no time before Aunt Julia called for her. Driving into their home block they saw Carla across the street walking toward her house.

"Oh, Aunt Julia, can you stop? I want to tell them about that dog."

Brian was already home and listened attentively.

Carla cried, "Oh, I'm thrilled. Wouldn't I have loved to see that miserable dog scared off! And I can believe Diamond could do it."

"Sunny, do you really think," put in Brian, "the boss will let me ride Starlight?"

"I sure thought his 'maybe' sounded like 'yes.' "

Carla questioned, "Do you suppose now, for a while anyway, that dog will stop running out at horses? We do love to go over the Big Bend."

"Better take Diamond along," advised her brother. "Looks to me, Sunny, as if you're going to be in demand as a rider."

Sunny was still smiling as she left them and hurried home to have time to change before dinner. She met her uncle in front of the house and he had to be told immediately of Diamond's feat. He joined in her pleasure.

But when they were inside the house, another atmosphere blotted smiles from their faces.

"Oh, Joe," his sister whispered to him, "I found Mother in tears when I got home. She clung and clung to me—so glad to have me back. She gets so unhappy alone. I was cruel to leave her so long. She's such a gentle, timid soul."

Uncle Joe made no answer, but his face grew more and more troubled. Later he said to Sunny, "I can't help it. It isn't right for Julia to be tied up here all the time."

"It's all fixed up," Sunny told him happily. *"Mere* Odette is going out with us. She was so interested in hearing how a horse protected a dog. She wants to see Black Diamond. We'll all go out together in the morning."

Sunny rode in the back seat with Beau. *Mere* Odette and Aunt Julia could visit in the front seat. She was glad to be free to think about Trot Inn, to plan her ride in the pasture, to ponder how Pal would treat Beau.

Each ignored the other. The truce of yesterday was gone. But once Sunny was mounted and headed for the pasture, she called to Pal. He responded with delighted bounds. It had been a dull morning, and he loved going with riders.

While she opened the gate, the dogs frisked about companionably, discussing smells. But Beau was keeping his eyes on her. He was ready to go through the gate the minute it swung wide. Suddenly he saw Pal duck under the wires at the side and race ahead. He stared after him for a moment in entranced delight, then dashed madly toward him, his tail flaunting his exuberant joy. So this was the way dogs handled gates in the country! Now he was one of the initiated.

6   The "Lights"

After her adventure of the day before, Sunny felt much more at ease on Black Diamond. They were old friends now. The day turned uncomfortably hot. Neither horse nor rider had much energy, so they loafed along, enjoying the out-of-doors.

Two dogs could uncover twice as much excitement as one, but even so the heat slowed them down. They hunted out one rabbit and chased it briefly. It went under the barbed-wire fence. Now it was on somebody else's land, and Pal considered his duty done. The dogs waited lazily while Sunny finished circling some trees, then cut across to join her.

Sunny, for all their meandering, thought she was guiding Diamond until she saw a big milky weed ahead, a sort of wild lettuce. His interest in it was plain, so much so in fact that she was sure, without appearing to, the horse had led her to it.

Sunny was well aware it was not good form to let a horse eat while you were in the saddle, but he had been so good to her and he wanted it so. Impulsively she reigned him nearer it and loosened the reins so he could drop his head. He crunched with pleased, greedy delight. Sunny, conscience free, shared his pleasure. Why not? He had earned it.

In the rides alone that followed, they established a habit. Diamond never broke form until Sunny gave permission, but when he had located some favorite tidbit, either by smell or previous knowledge of such plants in the vicinity, he mouthed his bit so Sunny understood. Usually she did feel he needed rewarding and would let him eat.

Often the green tidbits were off to one side. He would not leave the path until she loosened the reins. Then he would gratefully make his way to them. And he would enjoy himself!

Only once was there more than he wanted to eat. That day he discovered a large patch of his favorite. Sunny, who by now had often groomed and outfitted him in the stable, was in no hurry, so she decided to make this really an occasion. She slipped his bit off and looped the reins around his neck. She still retained some hold of him, but his mouth was free to do justice to a prize feast.

He ate and ate. Suddenly, as if an invisible bell sounded in him, he jerked his head up. All interest in the savory greens was gone. To show his appreciation, he was as helpful as possible in getting his bit back on.

Sunny could not understand his stopping so abruptly, but plainly the wise horse knew when he had had enough. It was fortunate Diamond did not know how often she went a little too far with a box of candy and paid for it later.

Before remounting him, she gave an approving stroke along his neck. Much as Diamond disapproved of sappiness, she had found he liked the tribute of an occasional caress. Rides alone with him in the pasture brought them very close.

She never had to regret the decision made that first time he pleaded for a nibble. With another horse, her indulgence would probably have led to demands for more and more spoiling until all discipline was gone. With Diamond she built up a bank of gratitude that never failed to pay out when needed. She was always glad that that first afternoon she had decided he deserved spoiling.

The first time *Mere* Odette came out, Sunny did little actual riding, feeling she must hurry back. But her concern was wasted. Neither Aunt Julia nor *Mere* Odette was ready to start for home. They were watching Twilight's owner work her in the ring.

Mr. Donald had a mare, Midnight, who was the pride of Trot Inn. All her colts were spirited, shapely, well-gaited, and with good dispositions. Twilight was as shining black as her mother. Sunlight was a sorrel; so was Daylight, the latest. A man from another state had bought Sunlight and taken him away. Starlight, a deep roan, was owned by a woman who boarded her at Trot Inn, insisting she had the best riding horse in the world but she was frequently too busy to come out. This worried Mr. Donald but suited Brian to perfection. He had the pleasure of the rides she passed up.

Several of the "Lights" had won ribbons, but experts rated Twilight the most likely blue winner. Mr. Carlton had bought her as a colt and trained her himself. For the present he kept the mare at her old home and entered every horse show possible, however amateur, so Twilight would get experience, but he was looking ahead with high expectations to Denver's famous winter Stock Show. Then Twilight would have her chance in the big Coliseum arena.

Mr. Carlton was resting his mare by the side of the ring where Aunt Julia and *Mere* Odette were standing. Sunny, riding around looking for them, saw Mr. Carlton was using the ring, so she returned Diamond to his stall. Brian had told her all about Twilight and her owner's hopes for her. He had said that when possible Mr. Carlton liked to have the ring to himself when he worked her.

As she walked up, Beau very quiet at her heels, she heard her aunt exclaiming, "Think! Suppose you do win a blue ribbon?"

Mr. Carlton smiled. "I'll be mighty happy with a red. Or a yellow or white. Remember, owners send their entries from all over the United States."

"I still think she has a chance." Aunt Julia reached over the railing to give Twilight a timid pat on her shapely, rather delicate, black nose. All Midnight's colts were on the small side. Aunt Julia looked up at the rider to be certain he did not disapprove.

Instead Mr. Carlton reined the mare closer to the railing. "I want her used to people coming up," he explained. "Pet her all you want to."

"What I want is to see this little beauty win." Aunt Julia's plain face was alive with enthusiasm. "It would be wonderful to be in the Coliseum that night and see her get a ribbon."

"I'll have Mr. Donald let you know at what performance she shows."

"I'm sure my brother will take me. He never needs urging to go where there are horses."

All the way home it was clear where Aunt Julia's thoughts were. "Imagine the thrill he'll get winning a ribbon—and I'm sure he will with that horse. You haven't seen him riding her, have you, Sunny? He's marvelous."

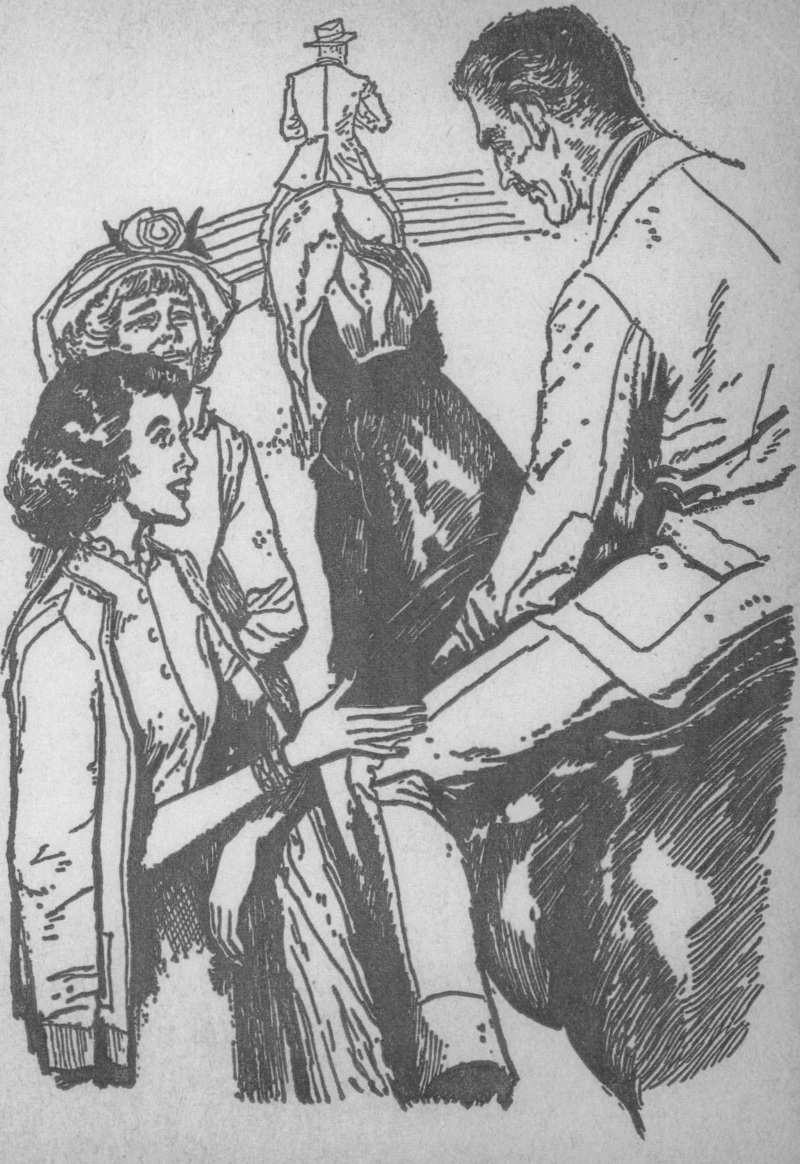

"No, I've always been out at the wrong hours. That's been nice because I've had the whole ring to myself. But I would like to see more riding."

"We should plan to leave you longer."

"Uncle is afraid I'm imposing on you too much already."

"Not a bit of it. But I think he wants to take you out himself tomorrow."

"He wants me to do only a little ring work and let Diamond rest up for a long ride Saturday with the others. He can bring me out long enough for that after office hours. He thinks he can make it early."

"I suppose I should stay home and get things done around the house," Aunt Julia agreed reluctantly. "I'll make that bread for you, Mother."

"It can wait," *Mere* Odette protested gently, yet with a hint of martyr resignation intimating it was as well the bread be made.

Aunt Julia spoke quickly, to change the subject before it grew disagreeable. "It's fortunate Joe's an engineer and works out his own schedules."

Mere Odette objected plaintively, "Had he been a

lawyer or doctor, as I wanted him to be, he would have no company at all over him to defer to. He would be on his own."

Aunt Julia turned a corner, then replied, "Most successful doctors and lawyers I know have few free hours of their own."

It was an endless argument, which Sunny had long ago heard echoed in her own home. Uncle Joe had originally wanted to be a doctor but took engineering instead so that when he left college he could support his mother and sister. From the first he had been successful.

Personally Sunny liked sandy-haired Uncle Joe exactly as he was. "He likes horses." That was all-important to Sunny. "I'm glad he thinks Diamond should have some exercise tomorrow. I couldn't go a whole day without seeing my honey."

Brian was home early enough to go out with them. "I worked last night till nearly nine and I'll have to tear over the minute I get home tomorrow. But I told 'em when I took the job that I had to have some Saturday mornings free."

Sunny sat in the back seat, partly to keep Beau company and partly so Uncle Joe would have more chance to talk to Brian.

She looked from one to the other, thinking there could not be two more different types physically. Brian was beginning to fill out his big frame, with a bit of swaggering satisfaction. His crew-cut hair was brown, of a shade that almost matched his eyes. Uncle Joe was very slight.

Sunny sighed, thinking of the assets boys wasted. They never gave a second thought to natural good looks. Her eyes went back and forth between the two in the front seat. They were so different, yet somehow she always thought of them as alike. Wait, the answer was easy. They both liked horses.

"Are you going to ride Starlight today?"

"I hope so. Unless her owner turns up. Sunny, how can she let some silly committee meeting last so long she can't come? And with a horse like Starlight to ride!"

Uncle Joe said dryly, "Maybe she doesn't call the committee silly. She's on rather important ones."

Brian retorted hotly, "I'll bet you wouldn't let any committee keep you away—that is, if you could ride."

"No, sirree," Sunny chimed in. "I know you wouldn't, Uncle Joe."

Previously Sunny had seen Starlight, the roan mare, only standing blanketed in her stall. Her charm was her dancing lightness. She was a dainty creature, a mare for a woman rider. Brian was fast outgrowing her, but she could still handle his weight.

Sunny gazed at her entranced, but once mounted on Diamond and beside the roan mare, she realized her own horse did not share her admiration. Wednesday Diamond had kept the young Daylight severely in line, but once the little filly behaved they had gone along together in pleasant companionship. He would have to endure Starlight, but he was not going to pretend to like her company.

He took his gaits with meticulous care. He was not a bit of fun. Starlight danced all over the ring, and he stepped aside for her. When she cantered her lead was wrong. Sunny started to call Brian's attention, then hesitated.

"Is she hard to handle?" she asked instead, as they slowed to a walk together.

"Sometimes. Her owner is crazy over her gaits. They sure are easy riding. So she gets away with murder most of the time."

"Like her lead?" Sunny asked significantly.

"I didn't notice. Was it wrong?" asked Brian carelessly. "You get to enjoying Starlight so much you don't pay enough attention."

"Is she ever shown?"

"Not that I ever heard of. Her owner has her for what she calls a 'pleasure horse.'"

Had Diamond just seen too much of this? Was that why he was so offish? It could be all her imagination, so she hesitated to mention it. It was the first time she had ever ridden with Brian, also the first time she had ridden with anyone in the ring. Maybe Diamond was this way with any horse in the ring.

She wished they were going outside. Since they stayed in, she was not sorry when Uncle Joe called that time was up.

7 *Put to the Test*

Brian's mother drove them out the next morning. Carla was riding with another, much smaller group. Sunny sat in the back seat with Brian, and she found herself telling him about Ruth.

A letter had been waiting when she reached home barely by dinnertime. She had tried to dress and read it at the same time, and she was preoccupied by it at the table. She had to talk about Ruth's problem.

Mère Odette and Aunt Julia could not see it as a problem. Her grandmother felt the sooner Ruth stopped trying to ride the better, and her aunt said she ought to do what she wanted to.

"That's exactly the trouble," Sunny burst out. "She wants to ride every bit as much as I do and you know that's plenty."

"Then there's no sense in being afraid. She'll get

over it eventually," said Uncle Joe.

"But, Uncle Joe, she doesn't. That's what's so crazy. She gets more and more scared."

"Can't that Colonel you talk about show her how to manage her horse better? Then she'll get along all right."

"You still don't understand. Ruth does ride beautifully. Her reins, her seat—all good. But she doesn't ride the heart and soul way she could if she wasn't afraid."

"I never heard of anything like that." Uncle Joe dismissed Ruth's problem, turning to subjects that seemed to him made more sense.

Sunny found Brian inclined to have the same views. "She ought to get over being afraid."

"That's what I'm telling you. She ought—ought—ought. But she can't. She goes right on being scared. She hasn't been bounced off again, but you know as well as I do how horses react to scared riders. She gets nowhere with them."

"So make her see how silly it is. She has to—if she really wants to ride."

Sunny sighed inwardly. Brian was no help. Yet surely there was a solution. Her best friend must not give up riding.

They passed through the gateway well on time, but riders were already congregating. Sunny looked them over eagerly. She hoped to ride often with many of them in the precious three weeks remaining.

In age, they were a more mixed group than she had expected. What counted, she soon realized, was the amount of their riding experience. Several today were starting with very little. Brian, his face beaming, led out Starlight.

Mr. Donald drew Sunny aside. "I'm putting a new boy on Ginger. He'll take care of him but Neva has been riding Ginger and there's no horse left for her but Pete. All the gentle horses have been promised. I think Neva can manage Pete but I'd feel better if, anyway, at first, you'd ride Diamond alongside of them. Pete'll behave then."

"I'd be glad to," Sunny agreed, flattered and elated at being asked. Diamond's rider was certainly never left on the sidelines.

The mounting went ahead with the usual difficulties, some horses standing patiently, others wheeling and fussing. As always a few riders had to yank reins and show authority in a fashion that often made Sunny wonder why even rental horses stood for it without protest, even though long inured to it. They could so easily buck off their riders. Of course they had training and discipline, but Sunny liked to believe in something even more in horses, something that Diamond had in excess—a sense of responsibility, of fairness in appreciation for the food and care given them.

At length everyone was ready to start. Brian was in the lead on Starlight. With her short legs, he could hold her slow enough for all her spirit and fussing. Sunny knew they were to walk for at least a mile.

She kept her eyes on Pete, staying a little behind where she could catch up if Neva had trouble. Neva was riding with a friend, and Sunny did not want to intrude unless it was necessary.

She found herself riding beside Kristy, who said, "I'd hoped to see more of you. Right in the same block. But Grandma's been sick and I've been there a lot."

"I hear she's better. I'm glad. It must be sort of spoiling your vacation fun."

"There's been a lot of dishwashing all right. My aunt gets all tired out and leaves theirs for me. With Moms working I'm supposed to do ours. But now Grandma's better I hope to get in more riding. Diamond's looking fine, isn't he?"

Sunny reached down to stroke his neck. "Mr. Donald says I can begin letting him out."

"And can he go! We all agree he deserves a rest— one rider. But we sure miss our turn at him."

"You're nice not being mad at my getting them all."

"It's only for a month. We can stand it that long. He dumped me off once. Has he you?"

Sunny shook her head. "I go easy on the reins and we get along fine. Kristy, isn't he wonderful to ride?"

"I'll say! Ha, here we are past the mile fence. We can trot now."

To Sunny's surprise they had left the ranch by the gateway and were on the public road. As the group broke into a trot they filled its width, but it was deserted at the moment.

Their swift pace soon brought them within sight of the house with the mean dog. Brian maneuvered Starlight back to her side.

"Ride up ahead, will you? There are so many of us, that dog may not come out but bring Diamond anyway. Mr. Donald says he scared the daylights out of the ornery dog the other day."

Sunny proudly urged Diamond to the front of the party. To a rider they were willing to slow down along here. If the dog was going to scare the horses, it would be easier if trouble started in a walk. Brian had difficulty holding Starlight behind, but Diamond led the group.

The dog was out. He raced toward them in a frenzy of barking. Then he saw Diamond.

He did not actually turn tail. He merely circled but the result took him homeward quickly. From a menace he became a disappearing coward. The riders whooped with glee.

Brian turned to Sunny with awe on his face. "The boss sure didn't exaggerate. Diamond has that bully's number."

As they again trotted ahead, Sunny could have stayed in the lead with Brian, a privileged position, but looking behind she saw Neva sawing Pete's reins. That would never do.

Sunny dropped back beside her. "Better loosen up," she advised. "He won't run away."

"He tried to. He wants to bolt off." Neva was obviously frightened.

"He only wants to make you think so." Sunny kept her voice matter of fact. That tone would convince and calm Neva more effectively than trying to reassure her that she was all right.

Actually with Pete she probably wasn't too safe, anyway, not if she kept on sawing at his reins. "Relax the reins—see?" Sunny moved hers slightly to show how loose they were. Diamond was understanding the need to slow Pete down, making no effort to pass him. His influence was wholly quieting.

Neva grew less afraid, and every gain in her steadiness steadied her horse, and every gain in steadiness in Pete steadied his rider. Finally Neva ceased to clutch the saddle and regained her seat. Before the trot ended she was riding almost in form.

"Good work," Sunny approved. "Just don't fight Pete. Let him go along with the group. And try not to grab hold of the saddle."

"I know I shouldn't," said Neva penitently. "It's so hard not to."

"I wanted to all the time at first," Sunny agreed. "But the sooner you can stop the better."

They turned off the road, going through a fence with a gate so easy to open that Sunny saw why Carla's friends preferred it. The Big Bend beyond was an ideal place for riding. A wide path topped a bank of an irrigation ditch, which kept water flowing by swinging in a gigantic circle across fields and pastures. Frequent cottonwood trees, their roots watered by seepage from the ditch, gave welcome shade. The mountains to the west were lightly veiled in midday haze.

Sunny had been told they could ride around the Bend, then cut back by a dirt county road seldom used. She rode beside Pete until she saw that Neva's troubles for the day were over. No set order of riders was long maintained. Pairs changed constantly.

Sunny let Diamond move ahead to faster and faster riders. Brian, in these safe stretches of the Bend, was giving Starlight her head. Sunny learned what Diamond's fast canter was like. For a short space she let him out, glorying in his speed and power, then she gently reined him in. Diamond knew as well as she did that it was wise to slow down. Gradually the party tapered to a walk.

Ahead she saw that Brian was not having equal success with Starlight. The mare too much enjoyed a romp. She was not actually running away, but she was rapidly outdistancing the group. Fortunately the other horses were not in a mood to race with her. The extra load of vacation riders had begun to slow them down, for all the extra oats and care given them. The farther Starlight left the party behind, the less she enjoyed herself. Brian finally had her walking. As soon as he could, he worked his way to Sunny's side.

"She's getting away from me. I haven't any business letting her. Look at her."

Sunny did not need to have her attention called to the mare's sweat-darkened coat. Mr. Donald was not going to be a bit happy when he saw it. "You'd better go very slow for a while," she advised, with a smile to take the edge off her advice.

"Don't I know it!" There was no answering smile on his face. "How can I, the way she's acting? She gets so excited with other horses. Her owner rides her alone or in very small parties, and not enough. Sunny, would you mind awfully turning around now and going back with me? I hate to be alone with her."

"Not a bit, Brian," she answered instantly. "I'd be glad to. I can leave Neva all right. She's doing fine now."

They explained his trouble to the others and turned the leadership over to Doug. Starlight wheeled in circles when Brian tried to turn her back. He at once dismounted and led her partly down the bank so the party could pass. Doug stayed behind to hold Starlight while he mounted.

Sunny felt Diamond's disapproval of the change but she was able to make him stand quietly to one side until the last rider had gone on. Then she discovered she had a real problem on her hands. Star-

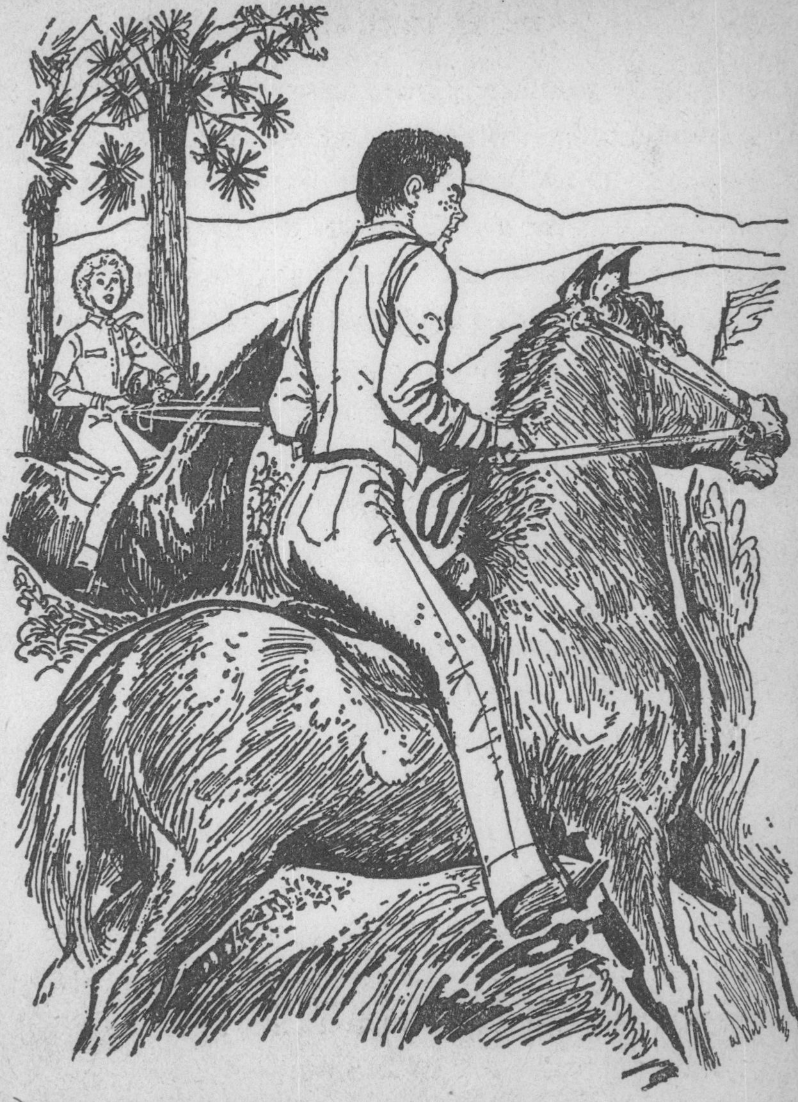

light, in the mood she was in, must not be passed.

Even in the lead, where the mare was pleased to be, Brian was not able to keep her from prancing and breaking into runs. Walking did not suit her at all. She wanted to show off before Diamond.

And Diamond, Sunny discovered, was not in the least willing to be an audience, to loiter behind. He wanted to show Starlight her place, which was far in his rear with a good view of his heels.

Sunny knew the horse had understood her perfectly when Pete needed steadying. Neva, a young green rider, was an old story to him, and whether Pete, a mere rental horse, was in front or behind him did not matter. Privileged Starlight, with Brian, an adequate rider on her, was another story. Diamond had thought Sunny an intelligent rider and she ought to see the difference. He became more and more out of sorts at being held back.

They returned the shortest way possible without going on a public road. Brian dared not risk Starlight there.

"And I thought she was such a swell horse. That

it was sweet for her to like her own way!" Brian was disgusted. "The boss can get somebody else to ride her after this."

Ahead of them was a gate, a wire one. "Whee, I wonder if I can get on again," said Brian.

"Don't try. I know Diamond will stretch out for me. If necessary I can jump up and sprawl into the stirrups. He'll let me. But I want to try that gate on him. He loves to help. Watch him."

It was a gate most riders dismounted to open, but Diamond edged very close so she could lift the loop handily over the holding post. She had to use her reins hand to steady the post that came free, resting the post on the ground till she could switch hands and hold it with the one that had lifted the loop. Diamond understood. He paid no attention to any loosening of the reins.

She gained a firm grip on the swinging post, which held the wires across the path. This was the tricky part. She had to keep on holding it and get Diamond around and through the gate without dropping it.

They made it, and she pulled the post well to one

side to give Brian a clear opening for Starlight. The mare had waited patiently for the gate to be opened. There was nothing else she could do. But once inside her home pasture she was ready for a romp toward the stable. She protested at being held back, wheeling in circles, while Diamond soberly cooperated with the serious business of closing the gate.

When that was done, the picture changed. Diamond knew he had done a fine job, entirely beyond Starlight's powers. He was proud of himself and his new mistress should be appreciating him, not making him take a back seat.

Sunny realized exactly how the horse felt but she was powerless. She must help Brian control that flighty mare. They had only about a mile to go. Brian finally convinced Starlight she must walk. Sunny came up beside him, careful not to deprive Starlight of her lead. Diamond grew more and more disgusted. His rider was sorry for him but helpless to change the order.

Suddenly Diamond stopped. Something was the matter. He wanted to get his head down. Was he choking on a bug? What was the matter with him?

She loosed the reins so he could take care of himself.

That was what he wanted. With his head free, he dropped to his knees.

"Look out!" cried Brian. "He's going to roll. Get his head up. Get off."

With Diamond already on the ground, her own feet touching earth, there was nothing she could do but step away from Diamond. Before she had sense enough to tighten her hold of the reins, Diamond yanked them out of her hands and was up and running. He had not dumped her, but he had certainly ceased to have her for a rider.

Brian started in pursuit, but she shrieked, "Don't! Don't race Starlight."

Brian pulled back on his reins with all his strength, stopping the mare. Sunny shouted, "Diamond's all right. He can't get out of this pasture."

Brian managed to circle Starlight back toward Sunny. "He's heading for the stable all right. What will you do?"

"Walk. It serves me right. But they won't know what to think, seeing Diamond tearing up riderless.

You get in quick and tell them I'm all right."

Later she learned that her horse had stopped "tearing" as soon as he was beyond them. Brian found him ambling along ahead and made no effort to overtake him, grateful that he need not excite the mare any more.

Sunny burned with humiliation. She had been taught often enough not to give a horse his head when he started to bend down. Watch out if you thought it was only for a drink. They might want to roll, maybe to rid themselves of stinging flies. She had never considered the possibility of Diamond's doing a thing like this to her, even with the provocation of Starlight. Yet Diamond had done it! Her Diamond! Wait till she got hold of him!

Brian and Mr. Donald both rushed to the gate to meet her. "You're sure you're not hurt?" Mr. Donald questioned anxiously.

"I didn't fall. I just stepped off. Where is Diamond?"

"In his stall. He's all right. Not even overheated. It's Starlight Rod's working on."

"So you think Diamond's all right?" Sunny raged.

"Deserves a nice comfortable stall and dinner after the way he treated me! Please take him out and saddle him as fast as you can. He's going to take me right back to that spot and tell me he's sorry. And walk at a crawl every step of the way home," she ended savagely. "While I tell him what I think of him."

Mr. Donald looked doubtful. "He won't be easy to handle. He won't like leaving his oats."

Sunny's eyes snapped. "He isn't the only one with likes. Please—bring him out."

"He did leave her feeling awfully silly," Brian said.

Mr. Donald laughed. "And he really shouldn't be allowed to get away with it. All right. If you think you can handle him we'll saddle him for you."

They were a minute or two getting him ready, and while they worked her rage began to ebb, and with it her brashness. It took all the courage she had to mount Diamond. She told him he should be ashamed of himself, but he did not appear to be.

As soon as Rod released his hold on the reins, the horse wheeled for the stable door. Rod grabbed hold again and forcefully led him several yards toward the gate, which Brian had run ahead to reopen. Rod stepped aside and Diamond continued on. But Sunny's relief was short.

Diamond came to a flat stop a yard before the gate. Sunny slapped him with the ends of her reins. Diamond moved—backward. Again she slapped him harder. He leaped to the side.

All at once Sunny's courage surged back. She had made a discovery. Diamond was doing his best to frighten her but not to unseat her. All right, let him try her out. She was not afraid now.

Brian, Rod, and Mr. Donald were in the background, watching with anxious faces. For another long minute Diamond put on a show of temper, then walked meekly through the gate. Sunny waved a triumphant "I'm on my way" to the onlookers, and walked a docile Diamond down the lane.

She did not say a word to the horse. Diamond needed no speech. But the riding bond between them conveyed all in light, carrying footsteps. Diamond had put her to the test, and she had not failed. She had not been afraid of him.

8   *A Present for Sunny*

Though Sunny loved her rides alone with Diamond and Beau in the pasture, she began going out much more with the other riders. Brian had a day off Tuesday, and Aunt Julia brought them out. They rode in the afternoon, instead of the morning, because Mr. Carlton had told Aunt Julia he would be working Twilight then.

"I've stopped worrying about imposing on you," Sunny told her aunt, "after both you and *Mere* Odette drove out Sunday in Uncle Joe's car."

Aunt Julia agreed with a laugh. "We came because we wanted to, all right. Mr. Carlton had said he'd bring out his ribbons. My, they're exciting! Just think of winning one! I'd burst with pride if I ever did."

"You'd better take up riding," suggested Brian, "and maybe you will."

"Me! On a horse?" cried Aunt Julia aghast. "Never."

Sunny was inclined to agree with her. Not even to win a blue ribbon. She changed the subject. "What horse are you going to ride today, Brian?"

He made a face. "Starlight. The boss asked me to see if I can make her behave in the pasture with just you around. He's been working on her."

Sunny sighed. Diamond did hate her so! But it did not prove to be too bad. Diamond had evidently decided it was up to him to accept the silly creature, and in the safe pasture Brian did not want Diamond kept behind. They were to trot together, and if Diamond got ahead, his mare had to learn to take it.

As a matter of fact, with her short legs, she had all she could do keeping up. She was compelled to work too hard to have energy left for foolishness.

They slowed down before she was tired or the least overheated. She had a good workout, and no more. Once down under the cottonwoods, they separated, Sunny showing Brian the game she played around the trees. Starlight failed to catch on to it as a game, but

Brian found it an ideal spot in which to work with the mare.

Tiring of her play, Sunny cantered Diamond away in a long slow circle, Beau with her. Pal had gone off somewhere with Rod, and Beau missed his companion, but he had done his best to explore the pasture on his own. Now he was entranced with Diamond's even pace and soon was racing along beside him, trying to match the canter with his own running lope.

Unfortunately he kept getting closer and closer to the hoofs. Sunny did not notice for she was fascinated by the sameness in their gaits. The horse swung around, jolting Sunny from her seat, and gave the dog a pushing kick. Beau yelped and fled. Diamond, worried over his bad behavior, tried to smooth his canter so Sunny could recover as easily as possible. He was waiting for a lecture.

"It's all right, Diamond. You didn't hurt him." Sunny knew this for Beau was running along with them, well to one side. "He had to learn not to come too close to horses and this was a good time to teach it to him."

She could see that Diamond was still bothered. He could not have dogs tripping him, but this one belonged to his mistress and he was responsible for its care.

The circle completed, Sunny rode over to tell Brian what had happened.

"I wish I'd had as much success knocking sense into Starlight," he grumbled.

"Right now I'd say she's behaving. I wish we didn't have to go in but time's up."

"Let's get a move on. I forgot to tell you the boss said Starlight's owner might be out later. I didn't know it, but Starlight scared her the last time she rode. She thought she was going to run away. So the boss has been working her all he can as well as sicking me on her."

"She should be fine now." Sunny studied the mare. "I hope her owner turns up to try her."

Aunt Julia met them at the stable door. Mr. Carlton was worrying that Twilight was having the ring too much to himself. He wanted them to ride with him.

As they were talking, a late model sports car drove

in and a pretty woman, attired in well-tailored riding togs, hurried out of it. Arliss Moore, Starlight's owner, had arrived.

Aunt Julia finished, saying, "He says Twilight needs to get used to horses jostling him."

Brian, rapidly dismounting, whispered to her, "He'll get his jostling now all right. They tell me Miss Moore lets Starlight get away with murder."

However a threatened runaway had sobered her down. "Is she behaving better today?" she asked Brian in a far from confident tone.

Mr. Donald was now on the scene. He answered for Brian. "Get on and try her. I'm sure you'll be pleased. The stirrups haven't needed changing so she's all ready for you." She had wanted her mare accustomed to the same bit and sadddle, so Brian had been using hers.

To please Mr. Carlton, Sunny stayed in her saddle, though she knew Diamond would not enjoy this kind of ring work after his romp in the pasture. It proved to be very sedate ring work. Twilight had lived his whole life around these same horses, and they failed to excite him. Starlight, grateful for a more lenient rider than she had been having, was in a mood to try to please her. Tension relaxed all around.

Mr. Donald had brought out a comfortable chair for *Mere* Odette and placed it near the gate, where she could watch the riders and still be able to talk to people. She enjoyed being in the middle of everything as much as did the horses. Everyone wanted to linger.

Dinner was very late that night, but Uncle Joe crunched some nuts and waited patiently. Sunny, thinking it a funny story, told about Brian's suggesting Aunt Julia take up riding to win a ribbon.

"I wish she would," he sighed. "So few ribbons have come her way. But I agree, I can't quite see her on a horse." He crunched some more nuts and said reflectively, "Did I tell you what she said when I objected to her staying home so much? That her mother wanted her and she could be of use around her and where else was she that? Sunny, she was always shy and plain and boys paid attention to other girls. She did get left out. But it's not fair because she got a bad start as a girl that her whole life has to be empty."

"Is that why she wants to win a ribbon so?"

Uncle Joe stood up, snapping his fingers. "I've got it. She's going to win a ribbon."

"Riding?" Sunny was sure he was crazy.

He looked down at her and laughed. "Well, no. But you wait and see. I'm going to fix it so she wins a lot of blue ribbons."

Sunny could not get anything more out of him by questions or coaxing.

"You wait and you'll see," he promised.

Wait she had to.

Thursday afternoon, Carla wanted to ride with a friend and neither had transportation. Aunt Julia readily agreed to take them out when she took Sunny. "But I don't like three in the front seat."

"Why do you need to?" Carla asked. "Brian has to work and can't go. There's just Joyce, Sunny, and me in the back seat and your mother in front with you."

"How about Beau?" asked Aunt Julia. "Where does he sit?"

Sunny could hardly contain her delight. "In back with us. Down by my knees."

"Joyce is as thin as I am. Maybe Beau can squeeze into the seat with us," said Carla.

Anyway he was going!

"Mr. Carlton may not be out," Sunny warned her aunt.

"He told me he would be," was the serene reply. "He's going to bring a cup he won. I did so want to see it."

Mr. Carlton probably far from minded showing it.

To Sunny's surprise, for she had expected to ride alone in the pasture, the older girls asked her to join them. Sunny suspected they wanted Diamond along to drive off the mean dog, but it was exciting to be seen with two older, experienced riders. She hoped nothing would happen to let her down in their estimation.

"How about Beau? He'll be so disappointed if we leave him behind. He did stay back Saturday but then he was with Uncle Joe. He never wants to leave him."

"Let him come," Carla offered. "He'll be all right."

"Won't he come too near the horses' heels?" worried Joyce.

Feeling grateful to Diamond, Sunny could promise

them they would have no trouble that way.

With Diamond along to keep away mean-dog trouble, they made the trip around the Big Bend. Coming back, Sunny told of having opened the difficult gate alone on Diamond when riding with Brian and later. So they returned that way.

They had started with the sun shining, but the sky was growing very dark. The girls hurried their horses to be home before it stormed. They waited impatiently for Sunny to close the gate, then they broke into a rapid trot toward the stable.

All at once lightning ripped across the sky, followed by thunder that seemed about to knock them down. Joyce's horse leaped into the air and plunged into a dead run, Carla's at his heels.

Sunny had not been out in a thunderstorm with Diamond and had no idea what to expect. She was thankful he did not bolt with the other horses, but she did long to reach the stable. Diamond had exactly the opposite idea. He went slower and slower. He turned into a stupid old plow horse who could not be urged to a faster pace. One slow foot came up and went down, then another plodding step. He kept in motion and that was all.

Sunny grew furious with him. There was no more lightning and only a few drops of rain. It was so silly staying out like this, waiting for the storm to burst on them. Wasn't Diamond ever going to make it back?

What would the girls be thinking of her? Probably that she was so silly scared she dared not try to keep up with them. Why, it was taking her nearly twenty minutes to cross the pasture!

She found the girls had put their horses in the stalls and they were over in the clubhouse helping Mr. Carlton build a fire in the fireplace. They were drenched to the skin and shivering with cold. They stared in amazement at Sunny, with her sweater only slightly damp.

"How come you're this dry?" demanded Carla in a piqued voice. She was usually the one to come through immaculate.

Mr. Carlton smiled down at Sunny. "I thought Diamond was keeping her out of any storm ahead of him. These girls rode through the very worst of it."

"We did that," Joyce agreed in a disgruntled tone. "Well, Sunny, you've seen how it can pour down on a house in one block, and our lawn, a block away, will not get a drop."

"But how did Diamond know about the storm?" Sunny puzzled.

"Animal sense. Smell or something," answered Mr. Carlton. "He wasn't going to ride into it even if the other horses did."

"Brr, I'm cold," shivered Carla. "Isn't this fire ever going to get hot?"

"Don't get too close to those burning logs," warned Mr. Carlton, "or you'll find out how hot clothes on fire are."

"I think it's wonderful how quick Mr. Carlton built it," praised Aunt Julia.

"You're dry." Carla was still shivering. "If you were wet to the skin it might not seem so quick."

The girls had taken off their sweaters, and the thinner garments next to their skin began slowly drying, but it was some time before they were comfortable enough to start for home. By then the sun was out.

The next day, Sunny was to meet Uncle Joe downtown for lunch. Usually he took her to quite a fancy place, and they had a deluxe meal. Today he took her to a lunch counter where the service was rapid. The food was good and filling, but not exciting. Sunny did not say anything but she was surprised. Of course, she should not expect him to continue the first elaborate treats forever.

Uncle Joe made no apologies for hurrying her. Once they were out of the place, he turned to the lower part of downtown, where she had not been before. The stores grew less and less attractive, some almost dingy.

Then he opened a door and led her into a saddle shop. Her opinion of everything changed at once. The drab became glamorous. She had never seen so many saddles in one place in her life.

Uncle Joe had obviously already talked with the owner of the shop. He had three dainty English saddles set apart. After studying Sunny's figure a moment he brought out still another.

"She is more slender than I expected."

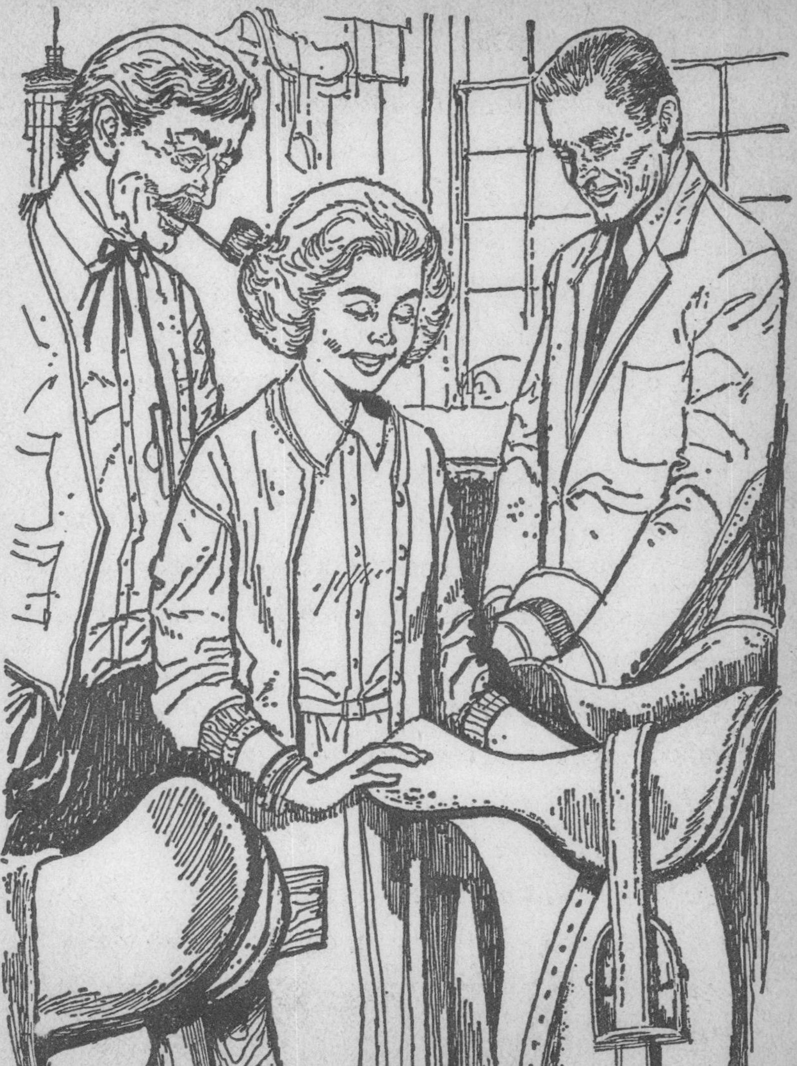

"Remember," Uncle Joe cautioned, "she's only thirteen. Still growing. I don't want her outgrowing it."

The man shook his head. "She won't this one. Anyway not till she's a grown woman. It is my choice for her."

He placed it over a low pole so Sunny could get astride it, though her skirt, pulled up all she dared, still gave her an awkward seat.

"I didn't know a saddle could feel so good," she told the man.

"Wait till you're actually on a horse and you'll know. And every day you ride in it, it will become more and more yours."

"That's why I wanted her to own one." Uncle Joe nodded with satisfaction. "So that's the one you pick for her?"

"I can tell enough without a horse. It will fit her." Being an expert, he knew.

Sunny's hand rubbed the fine leather with appreciation. "It must cost an awful lot of money," she said ruefully.

"It is one of our best saddles," the man admitted.

"She's one of my best nieces. I don't get to buy saddles often."

"Uncle, I thought we were playing window-shopping. You don't mean you are really going to buy it?"

He laughed at her. "Of course. This is one of the pleasures of making a good salary." He turned to the shopkeeper. "How about my driving by later and picking it up?"

"Oh, let me carry it home myself," Sunny begged. "I can handle it on the bus all right. It's not rush hours."

"I'll have it wrapped and you can see. You'll find it pretty big and clumsy," he warned.

"I'm lots stronger than I look," Sunny pleaded.

While the man was in the back of the store, Sunny stared about, entranced. Wonderful things for horses were on every side of her. Warm blankets and light ones. Riding crops. Western saddles. Lariats. Halters. All varieties of bridles.

Uncle Joe called her attention to a case of bits. He lifted out a snaffle bit, soft metal links that could go gently behind the horse's teeth, with rings to snap on reins. Here was none of the clamping hurt of a rigid bar with its center jut.

"Oh, how Diamond would love that!" breathed Sunny wistfully.

"I doubt if Mr. Donald would though. He wants Diamond sent out with curb control. A heavy one with many of the riders."

"You know Diamond could get away from me if he wanted to with the curbest bit there is. He wouldn't want to with one of these."

"You do trust that horse, don't you?"

Sunny put it squarely up to her uncle, "Wouldn't you if he treated you as he does me?"

"Let's buy the bit. It isn't expensive alone, and we'll use your old bridle till we see. You might try it in the ring. Surely Mr. Donald won't object to that."

The shopkeeper returned with the boxed saddle, a really big package.

"You can't take that on the bus," objected Uncle Joe. "I've got to get back to the office soon. First we'll go up and get my car at the garage. You can run in here and tell them to bring it out so I won't have to park.

I'll be ready to start for home with it in the trunk. I'll get there, Sunny, as fast as I can."

"I think she can live that long without it," put in the shopkeeper dryly.

"I know I sound silly," Sunny apologized. "But I'm still expecting to wake up and stop dreaming. And no saddle."

The men laughed.

"We'll be all ready to bring it out," said the shopkeeper.

"This bit, too. You have my address for charging, don't you?"

The man nodded, all smiles. It was a day that scattered smiles.

9   *The Contest*

Even before breakfast dishes were done, Uncle Joe appeared at the kitchen door, carrying the new saddle and bit.

Aunt Julia smiled at him. "You two kids! Sunny, run along. I can do those dishes. You make it up when time isn't so urgent."

Uncle Joe admitted, "I would like to get out before the place is crowded."

The wait to try the new saddle and bit had already seemed long to Sunny. Hurrah for Uncle for hurrying it up! "I'll call Brian and he'll be ready earlier."

Riding out, he sat in the back seat with Beau so he could examine the saddle. "It's tops all right. Does Sunny get to take it home with her?" he questioned enviously.

"It will fit any horse if you adjust the belly band,"

replied Uncle Joe. "Now Sunny has her own saddle to help her adjust to new horses."

"That will be wonderful, except that any horse with any saddle is going to seem no good after Diamond," said Sunny sadly, then brightened. "But I've still got a lot of rides left and now on my own saddle!"

Brian examined the snaffle bit curiously. "I've never ridden with one. The boss has one. I've seen him use it with colts to get them used to something in their mouths."

Uncle Joe said, not too confidently, "I'm going to ask him to let Sunny try it in the ring. Diamond can't run far there. I think he'll let her."

Fortunately they were so early that Rod, with the rental horses saddled and bridled in their stalls, had time to fuss, fitting the snaffle bit to Diamond's old bridle. Several buckles had to be undone and redone. Then Rod tried it in. Diamond mouthed it in surprise.

"A little tight." Rod redid two buckles.

Diamond's approval grew. He mouthed the bit with amazed satisfaction.

"See!" cried Sunny. "Uncle Joe, he does like it.

You see? I just knew he would."

"It's gentle with his tender mouth. But it sure takes away your control of him," commented Rod.

"Let's go over in the ring and see," suggested Uncle Joe.

The stirrups of the new saddle also had to be adjusted to Sunny's legs. She felt a trifle strange, for all her rides on Diamond had been in the same soft old saddle. She had grown more used to it than she realized. But the new one was not going to be hard to fit into. The man was right. It was her saddle. Let her just ride it enough to get its feeling.

Mr. Donald, who was always glad of an excuse to exercise Midnight, rode with her into the ring, half expecting trouble. Instead the horse appreciated a comfort his sensitive mouth had never known before. His reputation for willfulness had always seemed to require good curb control.

Sunny could feel him quietly mouthing the soft links, savoring gentleness happily. But he did not forget it was a bit, intended to convey orders to him. He was alert to her slightest use of it. Sunny had never had quicker responses from him.

Mr. Donald seeing that she was in control of her horse, put her through some snappy ring work, changing gaits, stopping abruptly, reversing, wheeling. Diamond never missed a cue.

Mr. Donald had to make it short. Saturday riders were arriving. Uncle Joe met them at the gate. "Looks like she can use it all right, doesn't it?"

"She can here in the ring but I still contend she has no real control."

"The horse did everything she asked," protested Uncle Joe.

"But he did not have a streak of not wanting to. She didn't try to make him do something he hates to."

Brian spoke up, "How about backing? He hates that."

"He took about three steps—no test."

"All right." Sunny was feeling very cocky. "I'll bet I could make him back clear across the ring."

"That would be something to make even Midnight do," Mr. Donald agreed.

"And you never question your control over her."

"Go ahead," pleaded Brian. "Have a backing contest."

Before anyone had time for second thoughts, or Mr. Donald could protest he lacked time, the lines and rules were set up. Toes scraped a starting line and the goal.

Both horses started willingly. A yard or two was easy going. Then both horses decided it was a silly idea. They fussed and objected. The riders began to need rein control along with every form of persuasion.

Sunny felt herself tightening up, as if literally her heart was coming into her throat. Diamond wanted to refuse her commands. Would he show up the bit's lack of control?

Not Diamond! He had approved and thanked her for its gentle comfort. He had accepted its authority. He continued to treat it as if it had curb power.

The unwilling backing went on, one backward step after another, each horse hating it. They were more than half across. Maybe the backing was no longer on a straight line, but it was movement backward.

A line of spectators had formed. It grew as more

riders arrived. If only her friends from the Timber Trail Farm were here to see her! If only Ruth were!

Then Midnight grew completely disgusted and refused to keep it up. Mr. Donald fought with her, curbing her sideways leaps, pulling down her upward rearing. But still Midnight would not move backward.

Diamond quickened his backward steps. With no more fussing, as if delighted to show his superiority, he backed faster and faster, over the line. The winner! The watchers clapped and shouted with glee. One their own age had beaten the Boss.

Sunny swung around to Mr. Donald. "Oh, why didn't you play fair? You let me win—cross alone."

"No. No. You were a real winner."

"You just want to make me feel good. The way you're always trying to build up us kids."

"Well, I've got to be seeing to those 'kids'. It's time you were all starting."

Not a word was said by anybody about changing bits. Sunny, on a horse still enjoying gentle links, rode off with the group.

She tried not to crowd her luck. Until she had used

the bit more she would not take chances on getting Diamond excited around other horses. She rode conservatively, but wonderfully in tune with her mount.

Her uncle said nothing to her until they were alone in the car going home. Friends were taking Brian later.

Uncle Joe's smile was broad. "Rod thinks it's a great joke. His boss admitted he simply could not get her back across the line."

Sunny looked incredulously at her uncle. "You mean Diamond really beat Midnight with Mr. Donald riding her?"

Uncle Joe nodded. "I do. But I liked the way you took it. Let's not have anything more said, but I am proud of your winning."

"I didn't. Diamond did."

"I don't think there will be any more objection to your using that bit." He turned to her quickly. "You didn't have any trouble out on the ride, did you?"

"Not a bit. I was careful. Some of them did a little crazy riding. If Diamond had wanted to act up he could have. Oh, Uncle, he loves that bit so he bends over backward trying to obey it and show how he likes it." Sunny laughed. "Didn't I use a silly expression for a horse? Bending over backward. Yet it does exactly describe how it feels as if he acted."

"Horse ways sometimes are hard to put into words," agreed Uncle Joe.

Sunny came back quickly, "Because we can't use horse language. Wait—I mean because horse language is not word language at all. But only silly idiots think they can't express themselves."

Uncle Joe turned his head briefly toward the back seat. "Beau, tell her how right she is."

Sunny, who had free hands, reached back to pet him, adding reflectively, "Maybe I'm not talking about horse language but four-footed language."

"And so many people who could not get anywhere in a four-footed world judge dogs not too smart when they do not react as people do in a people world."

"Uncle, I wish the people world had more of your understanding."

Uncle Joe, who never let anyone compliment him, changed the subject. "Who rides with you tomorrow?"

"Brian," replied Sunny happily. "I wish he didn't have a job. There are so many days he can't come out."

It was Wednesday evening that Uncle Joe brought home the exciting basket. He would not let Sunny or his mother peek inside. He carried it high in his arms, very carefully.

"I'll bet it's something alive," cried Sunny.

"We have one dog already. Oh, Joe, you don't need another."

"This is not for me." He was moving from them into the back hall. Sunny and *Mere* Odette trailed along. He went into the kitchen.

"Hi, Julia. Have you time to stop a minute and look at something?"

Her startled eyes went to the basket. "What have you got there?"

"Sit down. No, don't perch on that stool. Sit all the way down. You need a lap."

He rested the basket on the table and lifted out a mass of silky golden fur. Gently he held it toward her and shifted it into her arms. The frightened little creature trembled in her hold.

"Why, it's afraid. Have you been rough with it?" Instinctively she gathered it protectively to her, stroking it gently and speaking soothingly. She brushed back a mop of golden hair, and two great brown eyes looked into hers.

"Oh, you darling!" Aunt Julia cried, cuddling her closer with one hand, while the other worked its way in to the small broad head. Then a wee mouth opened and a very small lick was bestowed on the hand.

"Why, she likes me." Aunt Julia's reaction was delight.

Sunny was dazed. She had been so careful to keep any of Beau's loving licks out of Aunt Julia's sight. She turned to her uncle. "It's a Pekingese, isn't it?"

"She is Ku Wei Fe. Named for the Chinese Cleopatra. They spell it K-u W-e-i F-e but run it together so it sounds like Go away, Fay."

"Can I call her Kim for short?" Sunny questioned.

"I think her ladyship will permit it. She's soon to have puppies, and if they don't win blue ribbons you can stop believing in heredity. There are pages and pages in her papers—both for the daddy and her ladyship here."

"Puppies!" Aunt Julia exclaimed indignantly. "And you've been juggling her all over everywhere in that basket! How could you?"

Her brother answered meekly, "The kennels that sold her thought it was exactly the thing. Their most expensive. They say she is carrying her litter splendidly. In fine shape. She's been running everywhere around the kennels."

"Anyway she needs very special quarters here." She wheeled on Uncle Joe. "I take it you bought her. She is your property."

"Yours. Registered in your name. I took the chance you'd like her."

"As if anybody wouldn't! But, Joe, we haven't any preparations made for her care."

"Surely we've got some old blankets around."

"Old blankets! She needs the softest we own. We've got to take care of her."

Uncle Joe's eyes were twinkling. "The kennels gave me a supply of food to last till we can shop for more.

I think, Julia, we are going to be able to care for her adequately."

"Can I hold her while you fix her bed?" begged Sunny.

"And get dinner on the table," added Uncle Joe. "We are sort of hungry."

"Dinner," his sister repeated vaguely. "Oh, you said the kennels gave you food for her."

"She's had her meal for the night. Now how about us human beings? Whatever it is you've got on that stove smells good."

"Lamb stew. We had to use up the rest of the roast."

"You know lamb stew is my big favorite. How about letting me sample it?"

"Just as soon as we can fix a bed for Kim. I've remembered the nicest, softest old comforter we can use."

"I'll bring in that big carton from the garage. The one the new tank burner came in. Luckily we haven't burned it up yet and it's big."

"That will do. We can get something better soon. It's high enough so she can't get out and into harm.

We'll put it in the back room. Then we can hear her from the living room and the kitchen."

While she was arranging, and rearranging, the blankets in it, Uncle Joe called Beau in and let him smell the new bundle of fur very briefly. Aunt Julia was not sure she approved. "Hadn't we better keep them apart?"

"Maybe for the present," he agreed, walking Beau away and giving him attention elsewhere.

The dinner was practically ready, so Sunny and *Mere* Odette were able to get it on the table without Julia's help. Finally Kim was comfortably bestowed in the blankets, with water near, and the family was able to sit down to eat.

They had barely begun to enjoy the stew before there was a whimper from the back room. Aunt Julia sprang to her feet.

Her brother raised a protesting hand. "Now, listen, Julia. You can't spend twenty-four hours a day carrying Kim around. She has to get used to being alone some of the time. A little crying won't hurt her."

Aunt Julia had to agree. She resumed her seat but

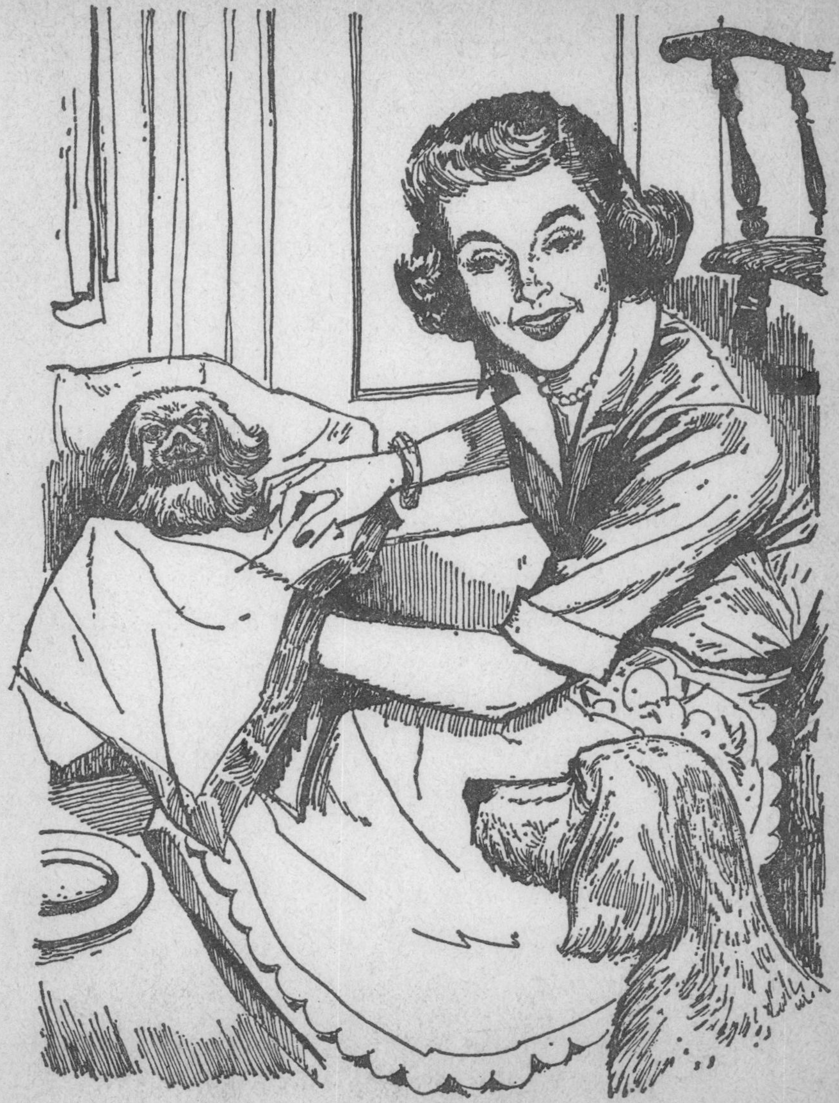

merely pecked at her food. The sad sobs continued in the other room. The meal became more and more an unhappy affair.

All at once the grieving ceased. "She's gone to sleep," said Uncle Joe in satisfaction.

"Let me see," Aunt Julia begged. "She stopped crying all at once. Something may be wrong."

"Go look. If it will satisfy you better to be sure she's asleep. But don't wake her up," he warned.

In a moment she was back with a glowing face. "You must come and see."

Mere Odette objected in a querulous tone, "We know a sleeping dog is sweet but come and eat your dinner. I want to eat mine."

"Sunny, you and Joe come. You've got to see him."

"Him! Kim's a her," corrected Uncle Joe.

"I know. Come."

Sunny led the trio. They paused at the door, their faces lighting with smiles. Beau had easily leaped over the barrier that jailed a whimpering Kim. He knew how to comfort her. He was stretched out, low to her level, so she could play with his ears.

Unfortunately he had kicked over the water dish. Aunt Julia brought in rags. "This is easily mopped up. We must fix it safer next time. Isn't Beau wonderful? Now Kim won't have to be alone at all. He will take care of her when I can't."

It was too much for Sunny. "Aunt Julia, they told me you didn't like dogs."

"Dog hairs do get on things," she admitted. "I guess I did object to Beau when Joe got him. But what's a mind good for if you can't change it?"

10 Uncle Joe's Bombshell

The next morning Kristy dashed across the street and skipped into the house. "Am I tickled! My aunt has fixed it so the owner will let me ride Pogo. Of course I can't take him over the bars but it's all right to do those logs in the pasture. I'm to stay in there. That's no hardship. I came over to see if you'll take me out."

"Gladly," Sunny cried. "Pogo! I can hardly believe it."

Kristy saw Kim in Aunt Julia's lap. "What's that?"

The proud owner lifted back a wisp of shawl, revealing a very combed and brushed dog reveling in the attentions her beautiful self was getting.

Sunny explained, "It's her ladyship, Ku Wei Fe. The Chinese Cleopatra. You should see her array of blue ribbons, and her pups are sure to win more for Aunt Julia."

"Blue ribbons!" gasped Kristy. "If I ever win one I think I'll faint for joy."

Sunny was amazed. Kristy caring that much! Blond, blue-eyed Kristy, who was always up in front, whose pretty ways pulled all the boys around her, who was always being queen of something or other. Surely she did not need ribbons to build up her self-confidence. But maybe nobody ever had enough spotlight. Maybe the more you had the more you craved.

Kristy had squatted down in front of Kim. Aunt Julia smoothed back the top hair, so the great brown eyes in the wide little face were visible. She allowed Kristy to give a few loving pats.

Sunny said, "We plan to leave about one thirty. Will that work for you?"

"Perfect."

"Uncle Joe is coming out to pick us up later."

"We didn't want to keep Kim out too long her first trip in the car with us," added Aunt Julia.

"Won't you ever leave her alone at home?"

"Alone?" Aunt Julia looked worried. "I'm afraid she'd be unhappy even if Mother stayed with her."

Then Aunt Julia bit her lips, fearing she might have offended. Sunny felt uncomfortable, too. *Mere* Odette had shown no signs of liking Kim, but until now nothing had been said.

Aunt Julia added quickly, "You see, Kristy, I think it's better Kim have the same person near her as much as possible. I plan to stay home all I can, for a few weeks, anyway."

Mere Odette regarded Kim with her first approval. She had not expected to gain an ally in this fashion. At least for some time in the future she would not be left in an empty house. Why, Kim could help her keep Julia home indefinitely. Her attitude toward the Pekingese changed completely.

With Aunt Julia driving, Sunny was allowed to carry Kim in the back seat, even though her mistress did wish Sunny had a little more lap. However, Kim cuddled contentedly against Sunny. Her eyes, though shaded by protecting hair, missed nothing. She was enjoying being enjoyed. Beau divided his attention between her and the open window beside him.

The first problem came when they parked at Trot

Inn. *Mere* Odette thought Kim would be better left inside the car.

"Alone?" faltered Aunt Julia. "Of course, I suppose Beau can stay with her."

"And miss his run with Diamond?" cried Sunny. "Oh, that isn't fair after he's been so sweet and good to Kim."

"You're right," Aunt Julia agreed. "He mustn't be kept back."

Mere Odette offered, as sufficient, "We can drop by every few minutes and see that she's all right."

Sunny had a picture of her remembering. Rod or someone would bring out a rocking chair to her favorite spot. She would open her knitting bag and, with the help of all near, untangle the yarn and discuss what a nice day it was.

Mr. Carlton was already in the ring on Twilight. Aunt Julia had promised to help him clock some of his gaits. "I think," she decided, "we'd better let Kim walk over with me. I can carry her if she gets tired. Though she is really very heavy for such a tiny bundle of fur."

Kim was delighted to be let down on the earth. Pal, to Aunt Julia's alarm, raced over. Beau gave a warning growl. Pal hesitated. Beau was on Pal's home grounds. Beau had guest privileges, no more, but Pal decided these might include the right to protect his small lady friend. Pal walked away.

Later, when the riders started for the pasture, he joined Beau for a most companionable hunt. Once their baying voices told of a rabbit's taking them in hot pursuit.

Before leaving for the pasture, the riders had been asked to join Mr. Carlton in the ring. Sunny gave willing cooperation with Diamond in drill work.

Kristy, on the other hand, had never paid attention to ring rules or its etiquette. Mr. Carlton turned sour looks on her. Sunny sensed his displeasure, which was wasted on Kristy, absorbed as she was in a first ride on Pogo, a mount far superior to her usual ones.

Sunny spoke so Kristy as well as Mr. Carlton could hear. "Kristy tells me her horse can jump logs. Later we're going to do it down in the pasture."

He welcomed the opportunity she gave him. "Why

don't you go at once? Before the horse is all tired out."

Pogo did not look as if that would be very soon, but both girls were delighted to be able to leave the restricting ring for the freedom of the pasture.

As they neared the creek, Kristy pointed to some fallen trees to one side of the lane. "You know, Diamond jumps. Not bars like Pogo, but I've seen him go sailing over big logs."

Excitement pricked at Sunny. Would he do it for her? She had never jumped anything on a horse. She'd try a small one first.

Kristy had no such plan in mind. Before Sunny knew what was happening she was cantering toward the biggest log in sight, and over it Pogo went. Diamond quickened his pace and followed. His light bounding leap gave Sunny a soaring sense of power.

Both horses carried ahead with the smoothest of canters.

Kristy turned a beaming face. "Couldn't you lick the whole world now?"

That was exactly the way Sunny felt. After a moment she said wistfully, "I thought you were ready anytime to lick the world. I never imagined you needed a jump first."

"Why do you say that?"

"All the things I hear come your way—honors, popularity, everything. Me, I'm always second."

"I don't believe that."

"Don't bother to be polite."

"You've certainly been taking the lead out here," Kristy pointed out.

Sunny blinked her eyes. She had heard Kristy all right. Then she knew. It had not been her. Diamond was the tops, and she had been riding him.

Before she could speak, Kristy exclaimed, "Look! See that log over there? I'm going to take it."

It was a big one. Pogo sailed over, but Sunny felt Diamond hesitate. It was a big jump for a horse not trained as a jumper. She did not urge him at it, but Diamond went forward, fast enough to put all his strength into a good, broad leap. He cleared it and that was all. He came down harder than before.

Sunny pulled him out of the following run, calling to Kristy, "I think Diamond's had enough. You know he's still supposed to be resting."

Kristy wheeled back toward her. "Just one more."

"You go ahead. Pogo's ready for a lot more. Diamond and I will amble around awhile."

As soon as Kristy, in search of more logs, was out of sight, Sunny dismounted and examined Diamond's feet. They seemed to be all right, but she would give him a complete rest for a few minutes. She slipped off his bit and let him enjoy the grass still green near the creek. She had found she did not need to retain a hold on his reins when she let him graze.

The dogs came up, checking on her, as was their habit. They stopped by a stump and sniffed with increasing excitement. Could it be a bird's nest?

Sunny called to them sharply. They reluctantly obeyed and came over to her. She played with them for a few minutes, till she hoped they had forgotten the stump. Then seeing Kristy and Pogo riding fast some distance away, she interested the dogs in chasing after them, while she went to investigate the stump.

Carefully she lifted the loose top and gazed down into a nest of baby mice. In her city home, a mouse had been something loathsome. These little gray fellows were part of nature's world, clean and appealing. The cowering mother's frightened eyes met hers. She was a creature afraid of Sunny with all her being, but equally she was determined to protect her babies as long as she could.

Sunny carefully replaced the top of their home, looked about to be sure the dogs were still safely interested elsewhere, and hoped the little family could be left in peace until they were ready to leave there. She saw to it that at least that day the dogs did not return near it.

Coming up to the stable, Sunny saw the green convertible. She looked at her watch in alarm, but they were not late. Uncle Joe was early.

"I've got more carrots in the car," she told Kristy as they neared the door. "I'll go get them and you see if Uncle's inside."

Rod came out for their horses. "Everybody's over in the ring," he told the girls.

Kristy begged, "Then can't we stay out a little longer?"

Rod, seeing that both horses were in good condition, willingly agreed, and the girls trotted over to the ring.

Sunny had expected her aunt and grandmother to have left long ago, but they were still here. *Mere* Odette's rocker had been placed near the gate, and the others were gathered around her.

Aunt Julia beckoned to Sunny. "You must hear this. Take Diamond over to the stable and hurry back."

Curiosity won over Sunny's desire for more riding, and she turned back. Kristy wanted both her curiosity satisfied and more riding. She kept Pogo moving toward the group, intending to listen on horseback.

Mr. Carlton rushed toward her with upraised hands. "You must not ride your horse so near the ladies."

Kristy looked around and saw Twilight tied inside the ring, many yards away. With a shrug she rushed Pogo across the yard after Diamond. Curiosity had won.

Aunt Julia's excited discovery was Mr. Carlton's knowledge of dog shows and of dog training for them.

"He says Pekingese never run in the ring. They are walked. Think of it!" She told Sunny, her face shining with delight, "He wants me to do all the showing myself. He is certain I can. And he'll help me."

"That will be a pleasure," Mr. Carlton insisted.

Uncle Joe said nothing. He did not need to. Obviously all was going to his complete satisfaction.

Mr. Carlton continued, "I do hope they have a puppy show while they are the best age."

"Where are the puppies?" Kristy asked in bewilderment. "I haven't seen any."

"They are not born yet," put in Uncle Joe dryly.

"Oh!" was all Kristy could find to say.

Sunny asked Mr. Carlton, "What do you think of Kim?"

He looked at the Pekingese resting against Aunt Julia's shoulder. "I should say a very, very superior specimen of the breed. I am trying to encourage your aunt to give it more exercise."

"She has been on her feet until just a few minutes ago," Aunt Julia protested. "I'll let her walk back to the car."

"I suppose we must be going," Mr. Carlton admitted reluctantly.

"There is so much more I do want you to tell me," said Aunt Julia.

Another date at the ring was promptly arranged. Sunny smiled to herself at how easily her transportation problem had been solved.

Sunny learned that Uncle Joe had been out at the stable some time, arriving soon after they left for the pasture. "A dull afternoon in the office and a pleasant place out here," he explained. He had been dividing his time between visiting with Mr. Donald, inspecting horses, and joining the party at the ring.

Mere Odette decided to drive home with her son, and parceling the passengers between the two cars took a little time. Aunt Julia was still driver, so Sunny must carry Kim.

"Why don't you sit beside me?" Then she could have Kim that much nearer her.

Beau had already been waiting beside the green convertible, and he leaped into the back seat when *Mere* Odette required his front one.

Kristy laughed. "Do I sit alone? Beau, how about my sharing with you?"

Beau hunched closer to the open window, leaving the side toward the closed window invitingly clear. They were all set at last.

It was not until they were eating their dessert that Uncle Joe fired his bombshell. "What do you think about my owning a horse? I bought Diamond today!"

"What?" came simultaneously from three throats with three gasps.

He enjoyed their surprise. "I've always wanted to own a horse. It's been a pleasure to see what private ownership has done to that black fellow. Mr. Donald feels as I do. The horse deserves more than being put back into the grind of rental work. A little rest has brought up his spirit and fire but it can't put real strength into him. A few weeks of everybody riding him and he'll be down again. Mr. Donald knows how everybody misses him, the attraction he is for the place. And all his present spirit will make the demand on him greater. It will be harder than ever not to let him out too much. So he's taking my offer to replace him with a younger, stronger horse. Of course that horse won't be another Diamond on the place. I know he's doing it mostly for the horse's sake, but in a way it makes sense for him, too. Diamond wouldn't last much longer at rental work."

Mere Odette asked in bewilderment, "You say that you are going to own him. You are not going to ride him, are you?"

"Me! What kind of rides could I give a horse?"

"Who will ride him after Sunny goes home?" asked Aunt Julia. "Her family doesn't seem willing to extend her time limit."

"It is getting mighty near the end," Sunny said sadly.

Uncle Joe smiled. "There's no law against a horse going visiting. Diamond might like to see what the state of Illinois is like."

"You mean have him a boarder at Timber Trail Farm?"

Uncle Joe nodded. "Something of the sort. You know anybody that would like to ride him around there?"

"Oh, Uncle! Can you really mean it? I don't have to

leave Diamond behind when I go?"

"Now, listen, Sunny. This is serious. As I said, Diamond is my horse now. This summer you've cared more about riding him than you've cared about anything else, but at home the situation is different. For one thing, you have your school activities."

"Uncle, as if anything could compare with the joy of riding Diamond!"

"That's what you think *now*. How about your pep club when the football games start?"

For a moment he had her stopped. It would be a sacrifice to give that up. She would if she had to, but it might not be necessary. "Pep club doesn't last all day. The Farm runs a bus. I can get out there at all sorts of hours."

"Starlight's owner has her own car. She can come any time. She's supposed to be wild about her horse. Starlight's been lucky in having Mr. Donald. He can't stand seeing any of his Lights neglected. And there is Pogo. I hear he's as badly neglected. Today his owner let a girl ride him when all he knew about her riding was that her aunt said she was good at it. I've had a lot of friends buy horses. Pleased as punch at the idea of having their own to ride—not a tired rental one. For a while everything is wonderful. Then things begin to interfere. So many things turn up that they want to do. They'll ride more next week to make up. And the poor horse stays in his stall. Oh, maybe a very fine one, but at best on a few feet square. The horse gets what exercise it has running circles at rope's end while the stableman has time to hold it."

"It would never be that way with Diamond and me." Sunny was very sure.

"All right. As long as it isn't, Diamond stays with you. I'll pay the bills. But he's yours to ride yourself—not to gloat over owning. Any off-the-scene ownership is confined to this end."

"I'm really to take him back with me?" Sunny still could not believe such good fortune was to be hers.

"As soon as I can arrange the best way to have him shipped."

Sunny ran around the table to fling her arms around her uncle. Tears were stinging her eyes. "Oh, I didn't know I could be this happy."

11   *Diamond Takes a Chance*

Sunny's mother believed in very firm mattresses for her family, and Sunny took it for granted all beds had that kind. At friends' slumber parties she slept on the floor, which was even harder. On trips anywhere they had camped out.

Her first night in Denver had been a real surprise. *Mere* Odette believed in comfort, and while she had not actually acquired a feather bed, the resemblance was close. Sunny, sinking down, down, had loved it. It made going to bed at the early hour *Mere* Odette set for thirteen-year-olds easier.

As usual, when the clock chimed, she turned to her granddaughter. Sunny rose obediently and going around to Uncle Joe kissed him goodnight. Then she paused and looked around. *Mere* Odette was waiting for her to "retire."

Sunny gave her uncle a half smile, saying wistfully, "I'm afraid to let you out of my sight. But it is real, isn't it? You do own Diamond."

"Silly child! Of course. You can go to sleep safely. I assure you I'll still own him tomorrow."

There was no sleep in Sunny. In this bed she sank, sank down. To turn over she slithered in softness. The more she could not go to sleep, the more she wanted to turn over. In a new position sleep might come.

Oh, dear, why had she ever liked this bed? If she could not get to sleep, time would never pass and she would never get to take Diamond back to Timber Trail Farm and Ruth. All her friends there would never see him.

She had been jealously hoarding every minute that was left of her visit, minutes riding her Diamond. Now all was changed. She would have days and weeks and months, even years, in which to ride him.

What a sensation Diamond would be at the Farm! She wanted to be off before anything could happen to change this magic plan. She could not leave soon enough. Making friends here had been fun, but think of riding Diamond beside Ruth! Savoring that, she slipped into sleep.

She was glad when no other rider wanted to go with her the next afternoon. Brian was at work. Kristy had other plans. In the morning Sunny grew afraid she might not get out herself. The day started exceptionally hot, then clouded over. Rain soon came in sheets, with sharp thunder and lightning.

Kim was terrified. Everyone gathered around her, forgetting their own fears in trying to reassure her. Beau, with soft nudging licks, offered her the only real comfort.

The storm was over as quickly as it started. Aunt Julia turned on the radio for reports of the damage done. Some streets were running curb to curb with water. A flood was rampaging down Cherry Creek.

"Trot Inn! Will it reach there?" cried Sunny.

"In the creek bottoms. Fortunately the stables, the ring, the buildings are on good high land. The storm didn't last long enough for flood water to collect and wash down the high land."

"Is it all over? So quick?"

Her aunt nodded. "We often have cloudbursts like this. It will dry up in no time except in a few flooded places."

Sunny brightened. "Then you think maybe I still have a chance to ride?"

"Your uncle wasn't planning to come for you until three. He'll see what it's like then."

Sunny went to the front door and looked out. The street was drying rapidly. Of course she shouldn't care so much now if she missed a ride, but somehow today she had especially wanted to be on Diamond.

If she told him about the coming changes, the horse could not be expected to follow words, but the way he sensed her feelings he would know something wonderfully good was in the air. Anyway she was going to tell him over and over that he was hers now, not for a month, but forever. He was really Uncle's, but she cared more about riding him than anything else, which meant he was hers forever. The smart old fellow would understand.

He came out of the stable all excitement. Could her feelings have reached him already? He had no patience at the gate. He failed to wait long enough, and the pole slipped away from her twice. She had to dismount to pick it up.

He fussed about orders to stretch out, but finally obeyed long enough for her to get her foot into the stirrup and spring over into her seat.

He gave her no opportunity for any sentimental conversation. He was all for trotting ahead as fast as she would permit. The storm had laid the dust and packed the sandy ground for perfect riding. He was not giving her his smoothest gaits but his most exciting.

As they neared the bottoms, she saw that the high waters had receded, but the marks of their passage were still plain. Old landmarks were washed away on every side; new ones set up.

Diamond's interest in every change was keen. She yielded to him and let him explore here and there. Once he took a tentative step forward, then reared backward. His leap almost unseated her. She remembered. Quicksand! Below that smooth surface might

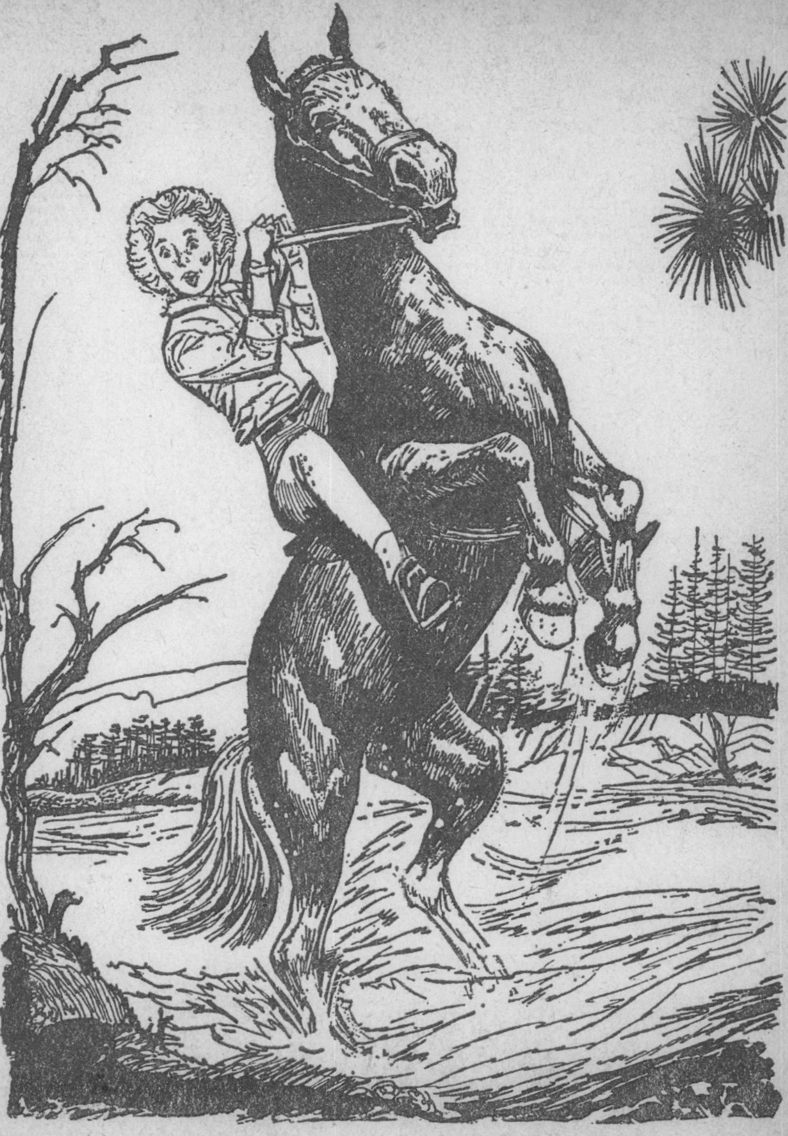

be the terribly dangerous quaking sand.

She was about to steer him away from the creek, but Diamond had other ideas. The instant he felt her secure in the saddle he gave a great bound forward, landing on much higher ground beyond.

Carefully he went ahead, exploring the changes in this section. Finally he was satisfied. He had seen enough and he let her turn him aside, but he still was the one to pick the path back to safety.

Sunny thought of Mr. Donald's warning, at a time when they were discussing bits, about Diamond's liking to go where he wanted to regardless. "Someday I'll find his rider's hat floating around and no other trace."

Sunny's hand went uncertainly to her head. She did not have even a hat to mark the spot. She had an idea the fellow had been taking real risks. Well, they were both still alive.

She rode around among the trees, enjoying the clear air and the rain-packed ground. She had a good ride, but she doubted if any of her delight in the coming changes had penetrated to Diamond. He had been wholly preoccupied with nature's upsets in his own small four-footed world.

Suddenly she had a worry. Would he miss all this and be homesick? She shook her head. The Farm was going to be all for his good, no more riders jerking reins to make his mouth sore, no more ride after ride till his feet gave out. No more waiting in slip stalls. Uncle planned to rent him a fine box stall. Wouldn't that be what mattered most?

Too, he loved attention, and her friends would give him plenty. The pasture belonged to his younger years. Another attempt to repeat this afternoon might not be so successful. He could find safer satisfactions. He'd enjoy being a sensation.

One more ride remained that would always stand out in Sunny's memory. Uncle Joe arranged for her to see a sunset at Trot Inn. He had often taken her to high points in town, a park or tall building, where she could watch the evening lights put on their pageant of changing colors among the ranges and high peaks, behind which the sun went down.

Once he had awakened her at dawn to see the snow-capped mountains glowing with delicate shades of reflected pink, like sheer nylon wear. She had often stayed late enough at Trot Inn to see the coming hint of sunset, but never more.

Now she was to stay till sunset's end. Uncle Joe was to pick up Brian after work, and the two riders would stay with their horses through the dinner hour. Aunt Julia would feed them both later, with an oven-kept meal in the kitchen.

Aunt Julia brought her out early. She had promised Mr. Carlton to help him again, timing Twilight's gaits. He had measured the exact distance around the ring and figured how many times was half a mile, attaching tags to show additional fractions needed to come out even.

Sunny hated not to bring out Diamond at once, but she knew it would be better for him to rest until Brian came. He was to ride Starlight, for Mr. Donald had the mare behaving much better. Diamond was not to pamper her by staying behind, and Brian was likely to set a lively pace.

"My brother," Aunt Julia told Mr. Carlton, "wants her to see at least one sunset in what he calls her four-footed world."

"It is worth staying for," he agreed. "So often while riding in the pasture I think of Tennyson's, 'I marked Him in the flowering of His field, But in His ways with men I find Him not.'"

Mr. Carlton was changing in Sunny's estimation from the so precise, so neat, not-exactly-sissy but somehow sort of dried-up, fussy old man. She had forgiven him these faults because he did love horses, but now she was discovering that in his own way he might be a better member of her four-footed world than some of the loose-sweatered, slacked, big fellows who made such a to-do about their sporting fondness for outdoor activities.

However, today it seemed to her Mr. Carlton was not giving Twilight his rightful share of attention. He rode some, but he stopped to talk to Aunt Julia even more. The way to blue ribbons, for horse or dog, seemed to need a great deal of planning, of discussion of means how and why.

Certainly Mr. Carlton did know about showing dogs. He was making Aunt Julia much wiser with Kim. She could not be kept from spoiling her, but after all, that was what those soft little pets were for. Kim would not thrive without a certain amount of spoiling, but it was fortunate Aunt Julia had Mr. Carlton to restrain her in some directions. Sunny was glad that carrots for Diamond did come in the same class as candy for Kim. Each one's begging fondness for a treat was hard to resist.

No matter what she was doing at Trot Inn, time always slipped away faster than seemed possible. Before she expected them, Brian and Uncle Joe were getting out of the green convertible. Beau had been beside the car door before anyone could open it. His Person had arrived.

Sunny smiled at his tail-wagged body. She said to Brian, "He's going to have a terrible time soon deciding whether to stay with us or go with Uncle Joe."

Already *Mere* Odette and Aunt Julia were getting settled in the car. Sunny was no longer in the back seat to hold Kim, but the little dog curled very contentedly on the wide seat next to Aunt Julia. Fortunately *Mere* Odette beside the window did not need more room.

Uncle Joe waved to Sunny. "Julia tells me she has dinner all ready. I'd best be starting on." He opened his door. Beau gave a startled look about. Rod was bringing out the horses. A ride was ahead. But Uncle Joe was not staying.

His master tried to help him. "Go on, old fellow, if you want to. I'll be out later to bring you home."

No, he was going where his Person had business and he might be needed. Sunny's heart warmed. She was taking Diamond home with her and she had been bothered at leaving Beau behind when he so delighted in their rides together. She thought of how often she had felt the soft push down of his nose and looked into his great heavily fringed eyes trying to tell her he loved her. Yes, he did, but now she saw how the core of his being belonged to Uncle Joe. He would never want to leave his Person, not even to come with Diamond to visit her. Rides were fun, being with Uncle Joe was his supreme contentment.

Brian and Sunny rode through the gate while the sun was still well above the mountain-tipped horizon, but they decided to stay within the home pasture, where Brian took fewer chances with Starlight.

Sunny loved to play among the cottonwoods, wheeling in exact formations, then swinging out in great figure eights, or cantering ahead, chasing sun shadows. Steadily the shadows were lengthening.

The magic in light was transforming the scene. The late sun rays glinted across shining grass patches in new splendor. Elongated, shadowy objects assumed strange shapes.

Again the light changed, giving a sharp clarity to outlines, while at the same time endowing the whole atmosphere with a mellow feeling of peace.

Clouds in the sky began to take on pink hues. Their random riding had them following a cow trail along a fence. Ahead an owl perched on a top wire of it. They stopped to look him over. They had no dogs to disturb him. Pal, missing Beau, had decided he was more interested in his dinner than in going with the riders.

The owl, without moving any other part of his body,

swiveled his head to stare at them out of unblinking eyes. The sunlight that blinded him by day was gone. Sunny was so fascinated by this near view that she wanted to stay looking and looking. Starlight could see no sense in delay. Finally Brian had to give in and let her move ahead.

The owl still kept a motionless body except for its head, which in a disjointed fashion swiveled independently to follow their passage in front of him. They left him perched where they had first seen him, only now with head turned almost completely around.

The path led back to the creek bottoms. Here the recent cloudburst had cut a deeper stream bed, pulling into it the water from several old rivulets. As they approached the bank through scrubby bushes, Diamond gripped his bit and nosed inward. Usually, riding with anyone else, Sunny did not let him eat, but they had been going through so many of their plays alone and he at least wanted her to know of a treat nearby.

She called to Brian, "Let's see what Diamond has found over that way."

"What do you mean found?" Brian demanded, looking about and seeing nothing.

"Maybe I mean smelled." She let Diamond pick his own path, and Brian, curious, followed.

They pushed their way through the bushes to the bank, very high at this point. Beyond they saw a stump uprooted in the storm. On its level trunk another owl was perched, or maybe the same one, for an owl could move about.

Sunny insisted later to Brian that this was what Diamond had led them to see. She did let him eat some of his favorite lettucelike plant, but, as she argued, they had bypassed plenty more of it with no owl near. Brian agreed Diamond did know the first owl had excited her, and maybe, just maybe, she was right. Anyway rehashing it later, they found they had shared many of the same sensations at the time.

The owl had stayed on the stump. Looking at him, as they did from the bank of the creek, his motionless dark silhouette was against a pale sky, with light forecasting a moon soon to rise. Stretching beyond the owl were the sandy creek bottoms, with creviced banks more shadowily mysterious as the moon appeared.

Still as the owl itself, they watched, waited. Brian let Starlight eat, too, and the munching blended into nature's sounds. No human one intruded. In the eerie lighting, it was as if Diamond had taken them into an owl's world of legendary spirits.

The dusky spell of night deepened into darkness. The moon hid in drifting clouds. Without its light, the owl was harder and harder to see.

"We ought to go," sighed Brian. "Anyway I'm sure that owl has decided we're not wise enough to be accepted into its learned brotherhood."

"No," Sunny agreed, "I'm afraid even with Diamond's help we get no owl wisdom."

Goblins might dance here later, owl wisdom be propounded in grave council, but *after* they left.

"Rod'll be coming to look for us if we don't get back soon," said Brian.

12   *Sudden Ending*

The telephone call came as Sunny left the backyard where she had been playing ball with Beau and Kim. Kim's part consisted mostly of getting in the way. Beau accepted her as a legitimate handicap. He knocked her over as little as possible and still caught his balls brilliantly. Practice with Sunny had been increasing his skill.

Aunt Julia had bought a small soft ball for Kim which, if it did not roll more than a yard or two away, she condescended to walk after, usually taking some time to decide whether or not it was worth the bother of picking it up.

Today Sunny had come in to report that Kim, after the innumerable times she had seen Beau return his ball to Sunny, had concluded it was her duty to do something with hers. She had actually picked it up, but instead of taking it to Sunny she had carried it to the back porch and sat down waiting.

When she was lying down, the screen door moved over her head when it opened. If she was left out in the yard, Kim soon settled in front of the door, and there she stayed. Aunt Julia was certain she was in danger, that some day she would be hit, but no one could persuade Kim this was so. But then, as Sunny pointed out, Kim never did raise her head while anyone was opening the door, not till it was spread wide for her to enter.

The telephone rang three times before Sunny could reach it. To her amazement, the one calling was a friend of the family, Mrs. Lee, who lived near her home in Hartland.

"I'm here in Denver," Mrs. Lee explained. "Like you, I'm visiting relatives. I talked with your mother before I left. She was so happy when I offered to take you home with me Friday."

"But I'm not going till next week," objected Sunny.

"I know. Your mother is changing the reservations. She's writing to tell you what luck she has. If you have not heard from her yet, I wonder if I had not better talk to your aunt."

"She's upstairs. I'll get her in a minute."

Sunny welcomed time in which to collect her wits. She had thought she could not get home soon enough to tell Ruth and others at the Farm about Diamond, but there were plans of all kinds for the rest of her stay. Mrs. Lee talked about leaving Friday. She would tell her it could not be done.

But here was Aunt Julia on the phone, exclaiming how splendid it was, that they had been worrying about a thirteen-year-old traveling alone, even a girl as sensible as Sunny. Now they would be as relieved as her mother and the family in Hartland.

Sunny tried to pull at her arm. Finally she had her attention. "Aunt Julia! All the things we're going to do!"

"Yes, yes, Sunny. We'll talk about that later." Her mouth went back to the instrument. "Sunny is worrying about plans we had made. It is too bad. We'll try to crowd in all we can before Friday. You say the plane leaves after midnight. . . . Oh, we have to get used to planes leaving at wild hours. We'll have her out there all right. . . . We can't help you with transportation, can we?" There was a longer pause. "Why, we'd be glad to. It won't put us out at all for we'd be going with Sunny anyway."

The center of all the planning listened helplessly. So she was to leave Friday, tomorrow night. She was not to have a last ride with the group Saturday. She was not to have the honor of being included on a ride with Carla's friends. She was not to be around when Mr. Carlton came over Saturday evening to discuss the best place for Kim's permanent quarters in the house.

Of course, the little lady had pretty much picked out her own favorite spots all over the house, but the position of a definite nursery for the puppies should not be left to such random preferences. Not that Kim's were exactly random. She chose her chair with great deliberation, then the rest of the family used other ones.

The kitchen jutted so in one ell the sun came in mornings. *Mere* Odette had always enjoyed breakfast on a side table there. Now this interfered with a place in a pile of newspapers which Kim selected as a good one on which to wait while her mistress did her kitchen chores. *Mere* Odette agreed it really was a pity to disturb her. She could breakfast in another part of the kitchen just as well.

But the question of locating a nursery must not depend on whims. It had to be the best place in the house for the most efficient care of puppies, and Sunny was not to be here to see Mr. Carlton make his selection.

She was not to have a last lunch date with Uncle Joe. She was to be grabbed up and put on a plane willy-nilly Friday night. Why, that was less than thirty-six hours off! And Aunt Julia thought it was all just lovely! Sunny glowered at her as she turned from the telephone.

"Of course," Aunt Julia said regretfully, "it is too bad to cut your visit short."

Too bad! That was all. Sunny wanted to bang something off the table to smash on the floor, to yank the telephone off its wire and hurl it through the window. She didn't, of course, but not from lack of desire.

Aunt Julia smiled at her. "My dear, we'll really feel

much less worried about you. *Mere* Odette may even overlook your going by plane now."

The postman arrived at this moment to shatter her last hope of a stay. Mother had been able to arrange everything to her complete satisfaction. Sunny would leave tomorrow.

Aunt Julia hurried preparations for going out to Trot Inn. "I know you'll want to get in all the riding you can," she said.

Sunny was glad she had planned to ride alone today. She'd tell Diamond, and he could take her sailing over a lot of big logs to help level off her exasperation. Maybe if they went over enough, nothing else in the world would matter to her.

She had to admit that he did his best. She returned to the house almost cheerful, to hear Uncle Joe's news.

"I've found exactly the way to ship Diamond. A friend of mine is sending his mare East to show. The animal is valuable and he is sending a groom with her. He's delighted to cut down expenses by having the man look after two horses part of the way. He can as easily as one. The catch is the horse isn't going for a while."

"What!" cried Sunny. "Here I have to go days early and Diamond waits and waits and waits here!"

"I'm sorry about your visit being cut short but I am glad you have someone to take you. And, Sunny, I'm sure it won't be more than three weeks before he'll be ready to take Diamond."

"Three weeks!" wailed Sunny aghast. "I may be back in school by then."

"You weren't going to stop riding when school began," he reminded her significantly.

"I know. But three weeks! I thought we were never going to be separated again. Now I leave tomorrow night."

"You still have one more ride," he consoled her. "Now what else shall we plan?"

Sunny looked helplessly at him. How was it possible to crowd into twenty-four hours all that had been planned for more than four days?

Uncle Joe did a wonderful job of trying. First he arranged for Brian to have the day off.

"I'll try to get him a good horse and one Diamond likes better than Starlight."

Sunny was startled to realize he did not need to. The horses had been getting along remarkably well, the mare accepting the older horse's role as boss and Diamond rather liking the younger horse's verve and enthusiasm. "Oh, let's have Starlight for the last ride. And do you suppose Kristy could have Pogo again?"

"We'll try to fix it."

More jumping! She'd see Diamond stayed away from too big logs but, oh, the joy of sailing over the others! She wondered what Starlight would do.

Brian, warned of Pogo's jumping, had no idea what to expect. As always Starlight surprised them, this time by doing nothing. Pogo went over a small log first. Diamond made a play of it with a broad jump.

Starlight gave the log a disdainful look and walked carefully around it, her manner conveying that it was fortunate one horse had some sense.

Pogo and Diamond romped over a few more logs, then they left the pasture and rode around the Big Bend, returning by the house with the mean dog.

Beau and Pal were getting tired. They had lost interest in side excursions and were keeping close to the riders. But any concern for them was wasted. The bullying dog must have seen Diamond before any of them saw him, and he kept himself far out of sight.

It had been a long ride, yet Sunny approached the gateway reluctantly. She was not saying the good-bye to Diamond she had once dreaded, but three weeks was going to seem forever. Then, too, she would not be riding him again in these familiar fun spots. True, everyone told her she must come again next summer to visit Trot Inn. But then she would not have Diamond. Even the whole bunch of extra carrots Aunt Julia had supplied did not make saying good-bye much easier. Though she did leave Diamond looking mighty satisfied.

Uncle Joe had offered to take them all out to a fancy restaurant for a last celebration. Sunny knew her aunt would hate leaving Kim, even in Beau's care, as the time for her puppies to arrive was getting nearer and nearer. Anyway Sunny herself did not want to go out.

"One of your dinners will taste twice as good," she told Aunt Julia.

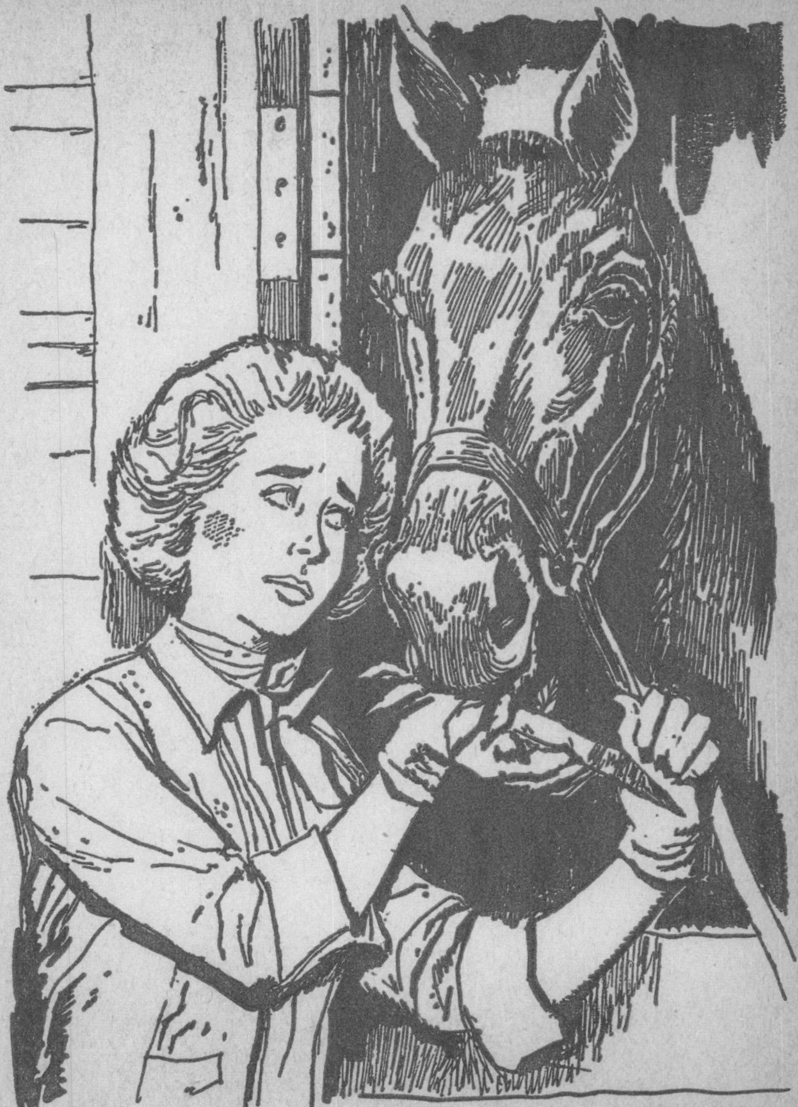

Queerly enough she wanted equally to stay with the old house. She was going to miss its roominess. In Hartland they lived in one of the new suburbs. They had wall-to-wall carpeting, floor-to-ceiling pole lights, long patterned drapes that could be pulled to cover an entire wall, or parted to make the patio sunshine part of the house. It was all new and lovely, but somehow she was reluctant to leave the spacious solidity of this old house for it.

The last evening was such a happy one. Beau had now become a settled part of every family gathering. With Kim here, *Mere* Odette had no more worries about keeping her daughter home with her, and Aunt Julia would soon have the puppies not only to fill the house but to bring a new world into it.

Blue ribbons galore! Aunt Julia was no longer receding into the past, French or otherwise; she was learning how exciting dogs could be. Tomorrow evening Mr. Carlton would be over to help her. She no longer needed Sunny's transportation to bring them together.

Sunny begged, "Send me some of the blue ribbons

so I can actually hold them. I'll mail them back registered mail to be sure they're safe."

It was time to leave for the airport incredibly soon. After much debate Aunt Julia decided perhaps Kim had had enough excitement for one day without going out in the car again. *Mere* Odette gratefully sank back in her chair. Kim was such a help!

Aunt Julia put an arm about Sunny. "You understand, don't you?"

"Oh, you mustn't leave Kim now. Anyway I like better saying good-bye to you here in private. I don't want to break down and cry out at the airport."

"I thought I was going to be the one doing that. Oh, Sunny, we've loved having you here."

Sunny returned her hug with a tighter one, then, feeling fussed, she broke away. In a moment she reached down to Kim for a last caress. "I did hope the puppies would come before I left, but Uncle Joe promises to take scads of pictures and send me every one."

When they picked up Mrs. Lee, Sunny moved to let her sit in front with Uncle Joe while she hugged

Beau against her. "You will miss me, won't you?" she asked him very quietly.

Her face got a good licking. She encouraged it. They did not have a dog at home. Her sister was allergic to dog hair. How awful if she herself had been!

The airport lights were ahead. One jet liner was landing far out. Soon their luggage was checked. Uncle Joe had to leave them at the entry gate. She had already left Beau in the car. She felt empty and forlorn.

Mrs. Lee insisted she sit by the window where she could look out, but the plane's wing kept her from seeing much.

Mrs. Lee made polite conversation. "I understand you had a very nice visit."

Sunny answered in an equally polite tone, "Oh, very."

If she said anything more she would begin to bawl. A very nice visit! What a way to describe the last month! But then who could? She had lived it.

The plane was taking off. When they landed, her father would be waiting for her, with their car in the parking lot. A long ride—then home.

13 *Big Plans*

Sunny's father was waiting first in line beside the exit gate. Tall as she was, Sunny was lifted off her feet in his embrace. She had forgotten what a great, big, wonderful father she did have. She clung and clung to him.

With her weight again on her own feet, he told her mock-severely, "Don't ever stay away this long again. We missed you too much."

He turned to greet Mrs. Lee. "My wife talked to your family. They're having car trouble so we convinced them not to risk a breakdown miles from help when we can bring you so easily. There's a whole empty seat in back if we three sit in front. Carol and Norman were coming—Ruth, too—"

"Ruth!" Sunny broke in, excited. "But you say the back seat is empty."

"I couldn't get away as early as I hoped. I had to crowd my driving so we thought it better for me to come alone." He turned to Mrs. Lee. "There's room for all the luggage you want."

"I haven't much. I only stayed a few days to see a sick brother. I'm glad I made the trip but I couldn't be away from my job any longer. It's grand you saved my husband the trip over if that generator is acting up again. I'm sure that's it. They just can't seem to fix it properly."

"They were about to send a wire that would reach you here warning you they expected to have trouble. But it's all arranged now. Let's get the luggage and be on our way."

Mrs. Lee suggested, "Let me take you to breakfast as a little thank you. They say the food is good at this airport."

Sunny scarcely knew if it was or not, or what was on her plate. She had eyes only for her father's face, attention only for his words. It was like meeting a new father, not the one she had always taken for granted as part of her background.

She was discovering that the best part of returning from a visit away was a new awareness. Away from home she had expected to look about and notice things, to learn why and how they happened. Sunny was grasping that she might have been a lot smarter if she had done this long ago.

Their home was like a new house to her. She kept exclaiming about how fresh and bright the drapes were, how lovely the sun shone through the big windows, pulling the outdoors, indoors. My, big windows were wonderful.

"Oh, Moms, we do have such a gay, happy house, don't we?"

Her mother beamed. "I thought you didn't like the upholstering we did last year."

"I love everything. It's all perfect."

Mother's lips quirked. "I'll have to send the rest of the family traveling more. I wish Carol shared your satisfaction in things as they are. Everything her friends buy she thinks we ought to have."

Carol did love pretty things. As sisters went, Sunny had never felt very close to her. Carol was two years older and attended a different school. What really made trouble was that Carol did not care about horses. And she thought pep clubs were sometimes undignified, and their suits cost too much when everyone else had one like yours. Carol loved to be the very first to appear with a new style or fad.

But seeing her again, Sunny realized how proud she would be to introduce her to Carla and her friends. If Carol went to Denver, Sunny was certain Aunt Julia would want her to go to that French society. It was nice to have a sister you could feel superior about.

Norman, her small brother, seized every minute she could spare him to hear about Beau.

"I love being home," Sunny confessed, "but I do miss him. Here we are with no dog at all!"

Their father laid down the evening newspaper he had been reading and turned to them. "I know it's tough, kids. I was heartsick myself when we had to put old Chief to sleep. But Doc was sure Carol could never be well in a house with a dog—even if we kept him in a kennel outside."

They both nodded. "Sure, we know Carol has to

come first. But she is so well now—" Sunny paused suggestively.

Her father shook his head. "She wouldn't be long with a dog around. But I know it's tough," he repeated. "That's why I've been making so many sacrifices to get you two out to the Farm."

"Daddy, will you ride Diamond when he comes?"

"Huh! I haven't been on a horse in years. I never rode much as a kid. My folks couldn't afford it."

"But riding Diamond won't cost you anything. Uncle pays his board bill. Daddy, you've no idea what riding him is like."

He laughed. "Diamond is in one class. All other horses in another."

"Exactly," Sunny agreed seriously. "The best part is he's safe for Norm to ride, too."

"Gee, can I?"

"Of course. The Colonel likes all beginners to try first in the indoor ring. Oh, Daddy, I wish you could have heard me trying to explain to Brian what an indoor ring is like. He bets Diamond is going to be surprised. He'd never heard of one with a roof except of course an indoor arena like the one in the Stock Show Coliseum."

"You know I'm not too good a rider yet," her brother reminded her. "You sure I'll be good enough for that horse? Uncle's Joe's picture of him was terrific."

"He is. And sweeter than sweet to small boys if you remember not to pull his reins. He won't stand for that."

"I wouldn't think of doing it. Not for anything. And, honestly, can I ride him?"

Sunny nodded with great positiveness. "If he ever— ever gets here."

Her father was surprised. "I understood he was to be here in about three weeks."

"Isn't that an eternity to wait?"

Ruth, anyway, agreed with her. "It does seem forever to wait. I'm so glad for you, Sunny, because it will make up for my being such a sissy."

Sunny whirled upon her. "What do you mean?"

"I'm sorry. I know you don't want me to stop riding but it's hopeless. I've decided definitely."

"It's just you *think* you can't," Sunny blazed at her. "That's the only trouble."

"All right. I believe you. But it's a big trouble. The horses seem to know I'm afraid. Oh, not so much of them as of my ability to ride them."

"But you love horses," Sunny expostulated. "You think they're wonderful."

"I know," Ruth agreed mournfully. "It's crazy. I can't explain it. Maybe it's because I do think they are so wonderful."

Sunny broke in, "Oh, I get you there. I never stop being surprised that Diamond wants me to boss him. Yet it's true. He's so proud of me when I prove I can."

"I guess that's it," said Ruth sadly. "Horses I ride are ashamed of me when I get scared of them."

"Then don't. You mustn't."

"I know I mustn't. But I do. So I'm going to stop riding. You won't miss me now that you have Diamond. I never could ride in his class."

Sunny grabbed her arm and held it hard. "You're going to ride him. Diamond himself."

Ruth stared at her aghast. "Have you gone crazy?"

"Not a bit of it. You have good hands. I was proud at Trot Inn when they said I had good hands. And I remembered yours. You always hold the reins right. Gently. That's what counts with Diamond. Even with a snaffle bit he won't stand for being yanked at."

"Listen, Sunny. Get this straight. I may have good hands but I am not a good rider."

Sunny's spirits lifted. "Wait till Diamond gets here." Somehow she was going to have to make him understand how important it was to convince Ruth she could ride him. Then when Ruth found herself successful with a horse as impressive as Diamond she would gain confidence. Diamond was sure to put on a good show to impress her.

Unluckily Ruth saw him first with Norman, a small boy, an inexperienced rider, in the saddle, and Diamond being very careful not to frighten him.

If only Ruth could have seen Diamond first on his arrival, all upset! The Colonel told Sunny later that they were certainly grateful her uncle had sent him in charge of an experienced groom. Even so, everyone had given a sigh of relief when he was in his stall.

School had already started before he reached the Farm, and Sunny had been in her classroom at the time. Her father had brought her out on a special trip to see Diamond that evening after office hours.

Sunny had a big bunch of carrots, but to her delight Diamond seemed even more interested in her than in her offering.

"Oh, Daddy, please, can't I take him once around the ring?" She did not have on riding clothes, but slacks would do.

Mr. Saunders' eyes consulted Colonel Dwyer's. "How about it?"

The Colonel hesitated. "I had thought it best for the horse to quiet down a day or two before anybody rode him. Now I see him with Sunny—well, we might try. I'll call a groom to saddle him."

Her saddle and bridle had arrived and were waiting in the tack room. "Please, let me saddle him myself?"

The Colonel looked dubious. "Don't forget he has had a most upsetting trip and maybe he isn't quite himself."

"Mr. Donald told me he hates being moved around in anything," Sunny admitted. "But he's here. And he's fine. Oh, thanks." She reached for the bridle.

Diamond helped her all he could, seeming delighted to be back in service, on his four feet, no longer being hauled here and there, or led by a halter. Instead of blowing out, a horse's neat trick to keep from having the belly band made tight, Diamond almost held in.

Soon she was again in the familiar saddle. Diamond, happy at being at work, seemed not to notice the difference between this indoor ring, with its heavy tanbark base, and his old outdoor ring. All that Sunny and Diamond knew was that they were again riding together. Walk . . . trot . . . canter. Round and round.

As they came out, the groom reached for Diamond's reins as casually as for any other horse's. Diamond in the Farm's estimation, had changed from the fighting black demon of his arrival to a well-mannered saddle gelding.

"He's standard bred," Sunny told her father. "Uncle tried to get papers but Mr. Donald said if there were any they had been lost long ago."

"He doesn't need them. All you need is to look at him."

"He's some horse," the Colonel agreed. He smiled at Sunny. "Now that you've introduced him to us, we know it."

"Diamond does hate to be made to do things he doesn't think he should," Sunny admitted. "Now he can stay put. No more moving."

Pete McCarthy, president of the Timber Trail Riders, and Dave Talbot, a boy from Texas who was living with the Dwyers in their pretty white house near the stable, had joined the men watching Sunny ride. Now Pete asked her, "Is he good at shows?"

"Wait till you see him! The only trouble is he knows all the calls and unless you're quick he gives away he's obeying them, not the rider."

Suddenly Pete's usually happy Irish face fell. "If we can't get him in a trailer how can we get him to the Horseshoe Show?"

The Colonel had the answer. "Someone can ride him over early enough to rest up. He'll be an asset to our entries, all right."

During the three weeks before Diamond arrived, Sunny had not come out to the Farm to ride. Rental horses were not for her now. But little as she had been out, she had heard enough about the Horseshoe Club event to know how exciting it was to be.

A neighboring academy had opened their show to outsiders. Soon entries had shown so much interest that the Horseshoe Club had expanded its plan to a community enterprise, and a large number of fine trophies had been donated.

There was one very handsome trophy for the club winning the most individual points. A blue ribbon added eight; a red, four, a yellow, two, and a white, one point.

As Sunny heard them praise Diamond, hope grew in her. Would it be possible to win, not only a ribbon but a blue one? To be, for once, not an "also-ran" but a first.

Norman and her father were, of course, sure she could. Her mother and Carol urged her to try hard.

"You've got three weeks to get Diamond used to his new home. He'll still be keyed up. In top form."

Carol said, "I'm going to try to get the doctor to give me shots so I can see you win." Horses were as bad for her to be around as dogs.

Sunny looked wistfully toward her. "Would you really care that much to see me win?"

"Of course," Carol insisted, being very casual about it now. But she had said she wanted to be there enough to take more of the shots she hated so.

Wouldn't they all be proud of her if she did win more than one blue ribbon? Blue ribbons. Exciting, exciting blue ribbons.

14 Ruth Meets Diamond

The Timber Trail Farm operated a bus to pick up riders, and Sunny planned to go out on the first trip Saturday. Norman wanted to go early, too, although his class did not ride until ten. Mr. Saunders had to work that Saturday, so on the way to his office he drove them across town where the bus could pick them up.

First Sunny had her own ride, in the indoor ring and in the outer one, and briefly out on the bridle path. Norman followed her, entranced, from ring to ring, but she left him behind on the path, so she soon returned. She caught up to him near the stable and leaped off Diamond with a swoop that brought her beside him. "Now you ride him."

Her brother's eyes grew big. "Now?" he gasped.

"We'd better go inside for your first ride." She put the reins in Norman's hand. "You lead him."

The ease with which Diamond followed reassured Norman. Sunny pulled a carrot from her pocket and gave it to Norman.

"He's got his bridle on," he protested.

"I'll wash it myself. I'm not going with the club on their ride. I want Diamond more rested before his first trip with them. I'll groom him while you have your lesson. Then I'll go back with your busload."

As Norman mounted, she cautioned, "Remember, no pulling on the reins."

He kept them too slack. Diamond would not like that, but Sunny saw the horse was gauging his rider and humoring him, not expecting proper horsemanship. Norman had a gleeful time. Finally he stopped beside Sunny, who had stayed inside the ring in case he had trouble. At this early hour, they were alone.

"Oh, he's the greatest. No wonder you talk about him all the time."

Sunny smiled. "Maybe I do too much. But I don't care. Go round a few more times."

"Can I gallop real fast?"

"Well, once around," Sunny conceded. It was twice

before she signaled him to slow to a walk.

The next moment she turned to find Ruth at her side. "How did you come to be here?" she demanded in surprise. "You told me you weren't riding."

"I'm not. The leaders in the summer crafts classes brought me out for a meeting in the lounge."

Sunny knew Ruth had served as counselor for a class in tile work, earning part of her riding fees.

Ruth went on, "I heard you had your new horse in the ring so I came to see you ride him."

"Norman's on him now."

There was no getting out of it. Ruth had to see Black Diamond first ambling around like any old rental horse, pleasing a small boy. He had found Norman could stick on him going fast and he had given him an exciting ride, but no one seeing him would ever suspect him of being a show horse. Norman brought out nothing of his style. Boiling with disgust, she had to stand silent beside Ruth, watching the ride.

Norman stopped again with a great flourish and climbed down. "Hey, Ruth! Did you see us go?"

Ruth turned in amazement to Sunny. "He really is

gentle, isn't he? Beautiful, too."

Sunny answered sadly, "And he can be some horse when he wants to. Let me ride him around once for you."

Norman left for his riding lesson, and Sunny proceded to put her horse through his paces with considerably more style, but the whole effect had been spoiled. If only Ruth could have seen him first, as she often had, insisting other horses make way for his prancing black importance. The horses yielded him a clear path all right.

There was something gained. It was going to be easier to get Ruth on his back, but being there was never going to inspire the confidence Sunny had hoped for. She would have to convince Ruth not only that Diamond accepted her as a rider, but that as a rider she could bring out the horse's best, as a small boy never could. But how—how could she make Ruth see it this way?

Wait! She did know of one convincing proof. If Ruth won a ribbon riding Diamond there was proof. Exactly! At the Horseshoe Show!

Elation filled Sunny. At long last she had found the solution to Ruth's problem. She would not say anything to her until she had ridden Diamond, but Sunny was no longer disappointed in Ruth's first view of him, for that dark cloud had turned inside out.

Yes, she had the answer to the problem that had worried her all her happy summer. Now she did not have to lose her riding pal, and Ruth was to find real joy in riding.

Sunny laid her plans carefully. There were going to be ticklish angles to persuading Ruth to compete. First she must ride Diamond. Today and Sunday were no days for the ride, with the Farm full of people.

Already a third busload had arrived, and the place was busier and busier. Ruth had to leave for her meeting in the lounge. Both rings were taken over with classes. While Sunny did not ride with her club, that did not prevent her showing off Diamond to all of them. Everyone on the bridle path exclaimed over him as she paraded him around. Diamond enjoyed their admiration as much as she did.

It seemed to her that Norman's group ended their

lesson almost as soon as they started. She had a few minutes, while they were drinking Cokes, to wash the carrots off Diamond's bit but she would have to groom him tomorrow. Luckily she had a long, free afternoon.

She persuaded Ruth to come out with her Monday after school. "I'll ride your horse around the ring a few times but you mustn't let me take up all your time."

"Just try him. That's all I'm asking."

Ruth, of course, was entranced with his gaits. She rode around many more times than she had planned to, hating to stop. Finally she drew up beside Sunny. "He's so easy to handle."

The Farm was so quiet Mondays that Sunny had not felt she must stay in the spectators' glassed-in section but had come into the ring itself. Now she reached for Diamond's reins and guided him so she could face Ruth.

She told her earnestly, "Don't you understand that ease is because you are riding him so well? Diamond loves to be ridden right, with an exceptionally gentle rein. You're just the type of rider he likes. I was sure of it even before I saw you on him. Now I know beyond a doubt."

"You're sweet to share him with me this way." Ruth's voice showed how pleased she really was.

"Haven't we always shared everything? Until riding started coming between us. Oh, Ruth, now it needn't. You've always wanted to ride."

"Haven't I proved that? The way I've kept trying and failing."

"Failing because you get scared and think you'll fail. Doesn't Diamond show you how silly you've been?"

"Anybody could ride him."

"I'll write back and have Mr. Donald send a list of the riders Diamond has dumped. Only he won't be able to remember half, the list is so long."

"Maybe he'll dump me."

Sunny shook her head, a gesture always emphatic and positive. Now it was even more so. "No. He won't. Not when you ride him as you did. He never has me and he won't you. You must see it. Same as we've always been alike, we're alike as riders."

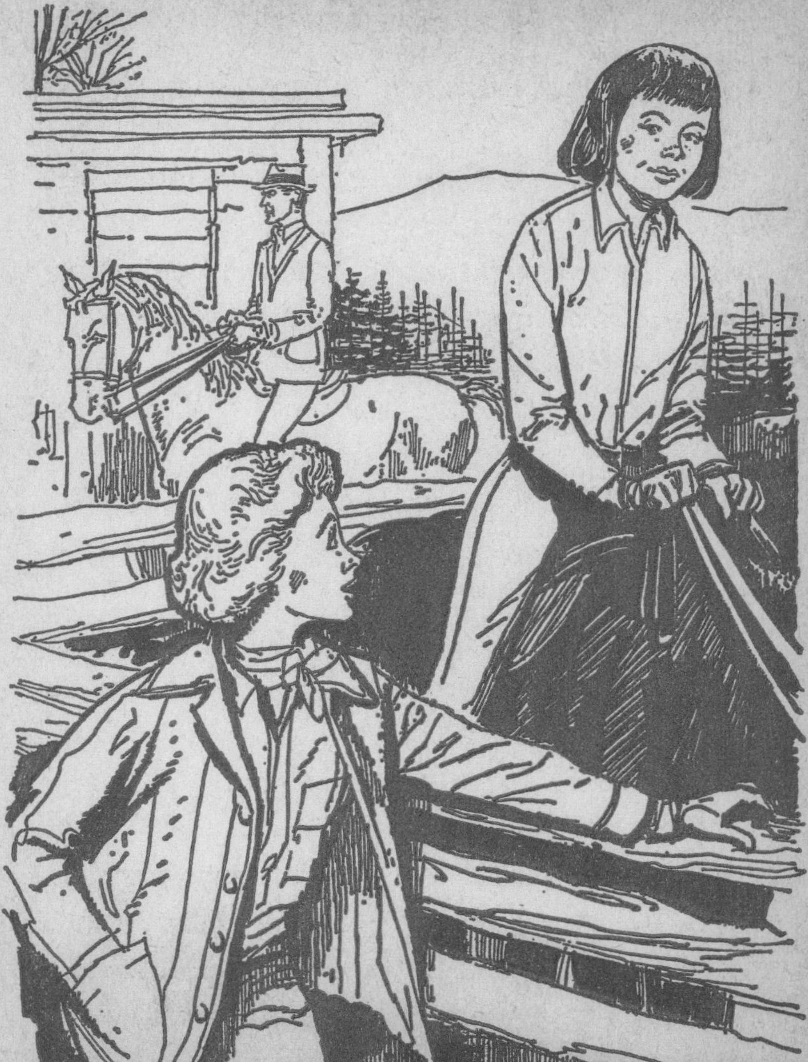

"I wish I could believe that. I've envied you your riding so."

"If you won a ribbon, you'd believe the judges knew you could ride better than the other entries."

"But I'll never win one."

"Please, for me, will you try just once on Diamond?"

Ruth bit her lip and looked down at her friend's pleading face. "Oh, I couldn't. Well, maybe. Someday. At a little bit of a show."

"At the Horseshoe Club Show," Sunny fired back.

"Oh, no!"

"Oh, yes!"

"It would be awful to make an exhibition of myself there."

"Ruth, you won't. Please, Ruth, I know you'll do all right and win a ribbon. Please try for me?"

"If I fail you will all be so ashamed of me."

"But you won't. I know. Do it for me."

Ruth slid off Diamond. "All right. I'll enter one number."

Sunny thrust out her hand. "That's a promise."

Ruth wanted to pull back. "I—I shouldn't."

"You should, too. You agreed to and you can't back out now. Shake."

Ruth yielded. Her hand had little grip but it met Sunny's. The promise was sealed.

Ruth said, "Now you'd better hurry and get your ride. The bus will be leaving before you know it."

"Diamond needs some exercise," Sunny agreed. "There were so many out the last two days I stayed close around here."

Now she wanted to show Diamond the whole bridle path and the side lanes. She had fun doing it, for Diamond was always curious and interested in anything new. He stepped right along, with good gaits, and held his head steady, but she could see he was not missing much. The orchards to one side were very different from his familiar cottonwoods.

He grew excited when he smelled water in the stream that ran through the Farm. They were allowed to let horses drink only with great discretion, but she knew she could trust Diamond. He would not start rolling with her on him, and a drink of running water was always a treat.

When he had all he wanted, she guided him to the bridle path and started on again. The approach to the bridge was thickly lined with bushes. They were on the bridge before they realized it. The hollow sound his hoofs made startled Diamond. For a moment, when he felt the difference of the bridge under him, Sunny thought he was going to rear. He stopped dead and pushed backward, unwilling to move forward.

"Silly boy," she scolded him. "I've been over this bridge a hundred times. It's perfectly safe."

Her voice reassured him. Still he started anxiously to inch backward. Sunny refused to let him. With reins and body she ordered straight ahead. Slowly, reluctantly, Diamond obeyed.

Finding nothing treacherous ahead, he regained his confidence, stepping with caution but with fast-lessening trepidation.

Once across, she was surprised to have Mr. Cleveland, on Gay-Day, overtake her. She had not realized she had had a spectator as she persuaded Diamond to cross the bridge.

"Mind if I ride along with you a bit?" he asked.

"Nice horse you have there."

It was something to receive praise from the owner of Gay-Day, blue ribbon winner at both professional and amateur shows. "Thank you." She lowered a free hand for a quick caress. "I think Diamond is tops but I'm pleased you do, too."

He was keeping Gay-Day in a lively trot. Diamond matched it, step for step as spirited.

"Shall we canter?"

Sunny nodded and took Diamond into the new gait, watching his lead carefully. It chimed in perfectly with Gay-Day's.

"Diamond likes your mare," Sunny expressed her pleasure. "I can tell so quickly."

"Can't you though! Gay-Day is a real nuisance when some friend of mine rides a horse she dislikes."

"Diamond disliked Starlight in Denver but he got over it."

"Sometime you must tell me how you managed it. Here's where we go in." He dismounted to open a white gate.

Intent on their riding, Sunny had not realized they

had completed the circle that brought them back to the stable.

"I had no idea we were so near home. It's a good thing. My friend is waiting. There were not many taking lessons this afternoon. The bus will probably be going soon."

Actually it was waiting for her. Diamond did not even get his farewell carrot.

The bus dropped Ruth before it did her, and she had no chance for more conversation with her. But then that did not matter. She had her promise.

Sunny was almost late for dinner. They were eating promptly as Dad had to be at some meeting early.

"I'm sorry, Mom, I'm so late. I meant to help."

"Carol was here so it was all right."

Carol nodded at her. "So you can be the one to do the dishes."

Sunny put up no argument. "I'll be glad to. I had such a wonderful afternoon. Ruth has promised to ride Diamond in the show."

Her mother raised her head, surprised. "I thought her mother told me she'd given up riding."

Sunny glowed. "Not now. I had her on Diamond and she agreed to try out at the show. Once she earns a ribbon she'll be over the idea she can't ride," Sunny ended triumphantly.

Her mother's face, so like Aunt Julia's, lighted with pleasure. "Martha will be pleased. She's been very unhappy about Ruth's not riding. She seems to think horseback riding is about as important as you and your father do, Sunny."

"Me, too." Norman was not to be left out.

Carol laughed. "Moms, you and I will have to stick together finding other things important, too."

Sunny did not even bother to ask what things. All-important in her eyes was her mother's pleasure in Ruth's promise. The two mothers had been friends long before their marriages. When they knew they were each to have a baby, likely in the same month, they had laughed about having a boy and a girl to grow up to marry each other. Two girls had spoiled that plan, but a close friendship between the two had pulled the families together almost as effectively.

"Oh, Sunny," her mother broke in, "I had a letter

from Julia today, in answer to about three of mine. She says to tell you Kim's puppies came and she's been too busy to write any of us. All three are fine and healthy. If you can believe her they are the most remarkable puppies ever born."

"Watch and see all the blue ribbons they win," Sunny crowed with delight.

Norman scowled. "Ribbons. Ribbons. That's all I hear. I thought you used ribbons to trim your dolls up."

"We did. And now, Norm," Sunny told him solemnly, "we use ribbons to pull people out of all the holes they get in."

"Who's in a hole?" Norman was a literal soul and this sort of conversation left him in the dark.

Mrs. Saunders smiled at Sunny. "You're getting wise beyond your years, my daughter. But you're right. Your Aunt Julia," she told Norman, "was in a hole being too much alone in a big house without friends her own age, and Ruth is in a hole being afraid of horses. Yet she's as eager to ride as her mother was."

"See?" Sunny grinned at him. "See what blue ribbons are for?"

15   *Sunny's Sacrifice*

Sunny's buoyant spirits received their first jolt the next afternoon when she talked to the Colonel and Pete McCarthy. They were not enthusiastic.

"Why waste a good horse on her?" Pete exploded indignantly.

Colonel Dwyer was on his side. "You see, Sunny, Ruth is really a poor rider."

"Only because she lacks confidence. This way she'll get it."

"How can you think she has a chance?" Pete demanded.

"Watch her ride Diamond and you'll see why."

"Then if Diamond can make a rider like her appear good, let's put one on him that will really pull up our score."

The Colonel put in ruefully, "I'm afraid the Farm

is not going to make much of a showing. I feel our Timber Trail Riders are as good if not better than most young riders, but many of the entries are from wealthy young people owning their own horses. I'm proud of your riding, Sunny, but even on Diamond you face hard competition."

"So why waste an entry on Ruth?" Pete pleaded.

"Oh, you two don't understand what a ribbon can mean to Ruth. She must have a chance to try. I know she'll do a lot better than you think."

The Colonel smiled. "You're a good friend of hers, Sunny."

"It isn't just that I'm her friend. Please, watch her ride him. She's coming out to practice a lot."

The Colonel put his hand on Pete's shoulder. "Let it go. If Sunny feels this way. . . . It's only one entry."

Pete scowled. "We need every one we can get."

"All right then. Get after that George Harkins. He forgets his lead every time. Are you sure he really understands how to swing in? Get busy with him. He's coming out for a group lesson this afternoon and I want you to take him off for some private drill."

The subject of Ruth was closed. They did not agree but they were not going to oppose her any longer. Sunny saddled Diamond soberly. Surely they would change when they saw Ruth ride. She was coming out Thursday afternoon.

As quickly as she could she rode Diamond away from everybody. She took the first side path, forgetting they were not supposed to use it. She thought it an ideal choice. It led through the orchard, and some of the trees needed pruning. She was kept alert, swinging aside from snagging branches. Once she had to duck low. The hazards added spice to the ride that Diamond enjoyed as much as she did. He was a good horse in the rings, but he loved the bridle paths best.

The Colonel and Pete's disapproval began to seem less and less important. Her ride made the whole world seem right. Of course she must not take away Ruth's chance. She must go on riding. Sunny knew they were wrong even if she could not make them see it. Besides, they had yet to watch Ruth on Diamond. Sunny returned home, her spirits not quite as high as they had been, but she was still in a cheerful mood.

Thursday's riding was completely satisfying. Ruth plainly enjoyed herself. The indoor ring was in use so they went to the outdoor one, where other riders made the going more interesting. But there were no classes there they would interfere with.

Sunny and Ruth were able to hold frequent conferences at the rail. Ruth was soon as involved in the finer points of ring work as Sunny had ever been.

Sunny hoped the Colonel or Pete would come around but they evidently were kept occupied elsewhere. They had to wait to see Ruth ride.

Ruth offered several times to let Sunny get in the saddle. "I will soon. First let's see you change to that trot again. Real smooth."

"I'll get it," Ruth cried. "Remember, you rode him a whole month before I did."

When Sunny finally did mount Diamond, she rode around the ring only twice before the warning bell sounded. The bus would leave in five minutes. Ruth was distressed.

"It's all right. I ride again tomorrow—Friday."

It was on Friday that Sunny was to get her second

big jolt. She did some of her homework riding out on the bus which carried only a small group of young beginners. She knew none of them.

Before taking Diamond out of his stall, she worked hard with brush and comb. It was a joy to see the black satin coat respond. The grooms, busy with beginners, had given her bare nods, aware she knew her way around now without them. Finally, satisfied with her job, she bridled and saddled him and led him toward the mounting block.

She saw Pete talking to Alan, a regular rider with the Timber Trail Club. She had noticed him watching Ruth ride the other day.

"Oh, Alan," she hurried up to them with delight, "tell Pete how grand Ruth rode."

It was then she saw the gloom on the boys' faces. Alan tried to meet her with a smile but it was anything but a gay one. "Yeah, she did fine."

"What's the matter? Is something wrong?"

They both nodded. Pete explained, "The Horseshoe Club has sure pulled a snide trick."

"You mean they aren't letting us enter?"

"Oh, they're letting us all right. But because it's to be on their grounds, they're making the rules."

"So what?"

"So they can win. They don't care anything about fair play, just so they keep the ribbons at home."

Sunny looked at them blankly. "It's been agreed that the judges be outsiders. You know the ones picked will be fair."

"Yeah. That was settled before the trophies were donated. Now they pull this rule."

"What is it?" Sunny demanded impatiently.

"No horse can be entered by a different rider in a different event. Same rider must ride the horse in all events where the horse is entered."

"Wh-what?" stammered Sunny. "They can't make that rule."

"They have. They've got many more kids who own their own horses. It's swell for them. Look what it's going to do to us—when we can't spread our good horses around."

Sunny stood stunned. Everything was reeling, but one horrible thought stood out. If Ruth rode, she couldn't. If she rode, Ruth couldn't.

"You can't let them get away with it!" she cried.

"Think we want to?" Pete asked. "The Colonel has talked to them. Other stables are mad, too, but most are not as hard hit as we are. The Horseshoe Club stands pat."

"How about the men running the academy?"

"We think they put the Club up to it. They claim the show is the Club's own idea—to have it on their grounds. These rules were planned for it."

"They let us know this rule mighty late," growled Alan.

"I'll say. But Colonel Dwyer says actually nobody had talked rules. We all took it for granted they'd be the same as for any show. A club can draw out—not compete—and that's about all. The rest are going ahead, mad or not. It makes us appear soreheads if we're the only ones to back out. Besides everybody wants to ride."

"How can we?"

"Use poorer horses, I suppose," Pete replied.

Alan turned to Sunny. "This sure lets Ruth out."

"Or me," mourned Sunny.

"Hey, none of that," cried Pete. "You've got to ride. Ruth might get by—win a yellow or white ribbon. You can do a lot better'n that. That horse your uncle gave you may save us from being last on the list."

"You two have no idea what it means to Ruth to ride and win any kind of ribbon."

"We know how we'll look if our club trails in last," cried Pete. "Be fair and think how the Colonel would like that."

"I've got to do a lot of thinking," Sunny answered in a broken voice. "Don't say anything about this—about Ruth riding—till I know what—Oh, dear, I don't know what to do." She turned blindly toward Diamond. "Let me ride. Maybe I can think straight then."

They opened the gate for her, out to the back bridle path. There she would meet fewer riders. Tears were streaming down her cheeks.

She could feel Diamond's sympathy. He was giving her his gentlest gaits, but lively ones, trying to divert and comfort her. He would never let anyone down.

In her heart of hearts she knew she had made her decision. She was not to have the glory of winning in the show. Its blue ribbons were not for her.

Pete thought she was letting the Colonel down if Ruth rode, but Sunny believed there was every chance that Ruth would ride beautifully, if she went on from her start yesterday. And if Ruth did not compete the chances were she would never ride much again. Moms would be on her side, or would be if she was not too afraid of making Sunny unhappy. It was a good thing she had Diamond to help her see straight. Ruth was to ride.

It did not take any time for her family to learn about the trouble. Her woebegone face gave it away, and they soon pulled the whole story from her.

Carol was furious. "You musn't make any such sacrifice. Why it . . . the whole show seemed planned as a chance for you to show off that horse of yours."

Her mother's face was very troubled. "She's right, Sunny. Of course it does mean a lot to Ruth but—"

Sunny broke in, " 'But' is ruled out. What it means to Ruth matters most. And that only. She's going to ride and she's going to win. Oh, in lots of entries. She'll have to go into every one she can to help on points. I may ride, too, if the Colonel can find a horse for me."

"You watch," exclaimed Norman, "there won't even be enough to go around our group. There is one class our age."

"I don't care. I'd really rather give all my time to watching Diamond."

"Go ahead," raged Carol. "Be noble if you insist. But I want *you* to ride."

"Just don't talk this way around Ruth," Sunny pleaded, "or you'll spoil everything."

"It needs spoiling. But I'll be a good girl, like my noble sister. I'll tell her how wonderfully she rides. Only I'm not going to take any shots to see her there."

"See what I saved you from." Sunny's laugh was not her liveliest but the family trailed her in it, and the atmosphere cleared some. Nobody was happy, but no one argued further with Sunny.

Word spread around, and several of the Timber Trail Riders who went to her school talked privately with Sunny. They were opposed to having Ruth ride,

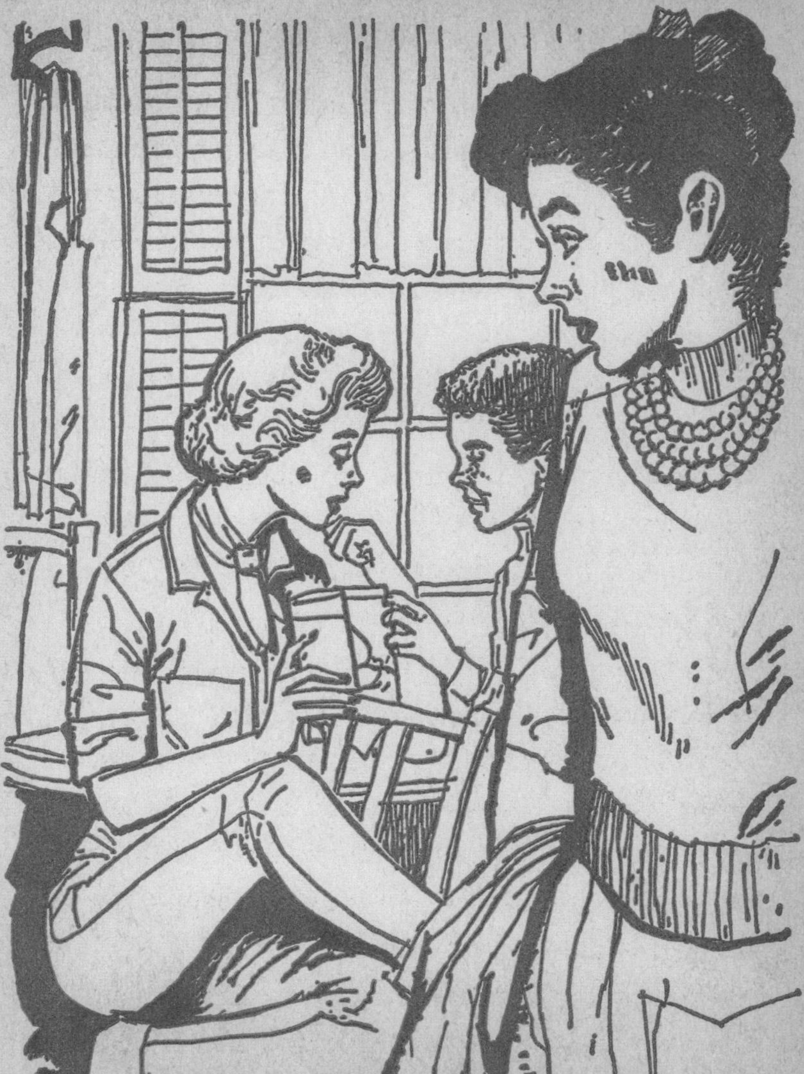

but if Sunny was determined to go through with it they promised to keep their feelings from Ruth. As Sunny pointed out, if they upset her, she would ride less well, so earn fewer points. She needed confidence built into her, not torn down.

Ruth did have to be told about the rule, that she must ride not in one entry but all possible. Sunny worried how to handle the telling. Then, in Social Studies, she got a break.

The year before, studying Africa, with another girl, who had since left town, Sunny had been very successful in constructing a model of a primitive village. They had used half coconut shells for dwellings. Pods from their trumpet vine opened into perfect native boats.

Today the teacher, Miss Cleeves, before the whole class, asked her to make a similar one. Ruth met her afterward with a beaming face. "Weren't you flattered! Especially when she said she's to have her exhibits displayed at the National Teachers' Convention?"

"I'd hate to disappoint her. But it will sure interfere with my riding. I'd been wondering what to do about this new rule but I guess this settles it. You'll have to do all the riding in the show."

"All the riding! What do you mean?"

Sunny explained about the unfair rule. "I'd been hating to tell you but—now this has come up."

"I couldn't do all that riding. I was to take Diamond for one entry while you won the others."

"You just said I must do that exhibit. I may never have such a chance again and you know how many shows come along."

"You can do both," Ruth protested.

Sunny knew in her heart she could. "You forget all the time I spent last year." She did not remind Ruth that many fumbling efforts need not be repeated. She knew now what was effective, what not. She added quickly, "I want to do it a lot better. It's going to take plenty of work. I need my mind free for it."

"It *is* an honor being asked to do it," Ruth admitted.

Sunny took her up quickly. "Then you will take over my riding for me?"

Ruth's face broke into a smile. "I hate to tell you how much I'm going to enjoy that chore. Riding Thursday—oh, I can't describe how it made me feel."

Sunny squeezed her hand. "Give up trying. I just know I feel equal to conquering the whole world."

"A wonderful world!" Ruth glowed.

"You ride. It was simply intended to be."

Sunny tried to keep on feeling that way, that it was good the rule gave Ruth all the entries, all these chances to prove her skill. She urged Ruth to ride Diamond as much as possible, get in all the practice she could. It was not so easy when Ruth took her literally and rode every afternoon and all the weekend.

Sunny went out with her sometimes, and Sunday she did squeeze in a wee ride of her own. But most of the time she stood by the rail and watched another girl ride her horse.

If Ruth did something her way, every part of her reached out to be in the saddle getting Diamond's responses. If Ruth worked a little differently, Sunny resented Diamond's complying. Why, maybe he even liked it different.

Sunny scolded herself for being a silly idiot, jealous this way. She wanted Ruth to be a success, didn't she? She knew any ribbons Ruth might win would bring results far more important than her satisfaction in a blue ribbon. Oh, her mind knew all right why she wanted Ruth to win.

Her exhibit at school was not taking second place to anything in the classrooms. If it was simply to be first in something she craved, why wasn't she more elated about it? She was proving, all right, that she was not entirely an "also-ran." So why this feeling of missing out? It was only temporary. She'd soon be again in the saddle, not a mere spectator.

She discovered another reason she was not happier. Her friends were avoiding her. Not pointedly. Not angrily. Rather as you swerve to avoid walking near something unpleasant. She understood their attitude. They did not want to make it an issue, or Ruth might catch on, be upset, enough anyway to spoil her riding. They wanted any points she might win.

It was Sunny's own horse, and they recognized her right to let her friend use it, but they thought she was not being quite fair to the Timber Trail Riders, not cooperating as she might have.

Pete did stop to talk to her one day. "She's doing

a lot better that I ever thought she could," he admitted grudgingly. "But it still isn't too late for you to change your mind. We hate making a poor showing. She may break any time."

He did not seem surprised when she shook her head. "She won't. It's all settled. Don't let's argue any more. But if you want me to, I can enter on some other horse —if there are any left."

He shook his head. "Not a one."

"I'm glad, for Ruth thinks that school exhibit needs all my time. She might be bothered if she found I was riding another horse."

"You know," he gave her a shadow of a smile, "Alan thinks you're doing right."

"He does!" There was nothing halfway about Sunny's pleasure. "I didn't know that."

"I didn't want you to." Even the shadow of a smile was banished by his scowl. "I'm still pulling for you to ride."

"No chance."

So someone—Alan!—thought she was doing right. A ray of cheer lightened the gloom.

16   *The Worst Possible Time*

Sunny stayed after school to work on her model. It was practically complete. Her final touches were very trivial, but they gave her something to do. She was not expected at home this early. Out at the Farm she would merely stand around, watching Ruth on Diamond, and pretend she did not see those around her. The truth was they did not want to notice her, and it was easier for everybody if she stayed away. Saturday was nearly here, and then it would all be over.

Miss Cleeves called to her that she was ready to close the room. She stopped by the model to praise it. Sunny tried to appear as pleased as she should be. Actually she had had to force her interest in building it, which had made her all the more conscientious trying to think up new features for it. This was a sad substitute for work toward a possible blue ribbon. She was glad to walk out of the room and leave the miniature village behind.

Her mother was home and, seeing her downcast face, tried to cheer her up. "Saturday is only two days off. It will soon be over."

Soon be over, soon be over rang in Sunny's ears with less and less consolation. Time was dragging so slowly. Sunday, when Diamond would again be her horse, was an eternity away.

Mrs. Saunders went on, "There's a letter for you from Denver. A big fat one."

Sunny raced to the desk to find it and tore it open, eager for news of Beau and the puppies. In a moment she was back to her mother, her face beaming with surprise.

"Moms! Aunt Julia and Mr. Carlton are getting married."

Mrs. Saunders was as astonished as she was. Separate sheets, in different handwritings, were spilling from Sunny's hands and she caught one letter, while Sunny read on in another.

Uncle Joe wrote he could not claim to be surprised,

for John Carlton had been coming over to the house almost daily to advise Julia about the puppies or to take her out to Trot Inn to see Twilight. "He might as well be living here. But they certainly are in a rush to get tied up."

Mrs. Saunders finished her sister's letter first, saying, "It does sound unbelievable. Julia marrying! And he sounds very suitable. Julia gives his family connections and his references as if she were hiring a maid."

"Uncle Joe says she is so happy she's as pretty as a young girl. And he seems to like Mr. Carlton."

"You met him, Sunny. Do you like him?"

"He's all right. Sort of a fussy old fellow. But a good rider," she added hastily.

"How will he fit in? Julia writes they will continue living where they are. There is no question to it. He thinks it an ideal house for puppies. *That* seems to settle it." Mrs. Saunders did not know whether to laugh or groan.

"Moms, you simply don't understand how important those puppies are. They may sell for fabulous prices and Aunt Julia is so proud of being Kim's owner. Ku

Wei Fe really is something. Besides, don't you see it's the puppies that brought them together? That and Aunt Julia's finding Twilight so remarkable and so sure to win blue ribbons."

"You've got something there," her mother admitted with a smile. "It is, of course, the bond that brought them together. So I suppose it's natural for them to make a fuss over the puppies."

"Moms, they ought to. Oh, I'd like to see them."

"How about my mother? I am so happy they will stay in that house she clings to. But will she get along with him?"

"Mr. Carlton is lovely to her. Really sweet. She'll be so much happier with him there all the time. Aunt Julia can have fun of her own without leaving her out."

"I declare, Sunny, none of it is as unlikely as it sounds. That Ku Wei Fe has worked wonders."

"Moms, the four-footed world always does if you leave it to them."

"All right, my young fanatic, the arguments are all yours today. Now read Julia's letter and give me Joe's."

Suddenly Mrs. Saunders burst out, "Sunny, didn't you miss this page? Did you realize Joe may come to visit us soon?"

"What? I didn't see that. When?"

"You must have missed this whole page. Listen. 'They want to be married very soon. I can't set a date for my trip until the company knows when the man I have to see will be in Chicago. I may be able to run over for a day with you folks. We've missed you, Sunny. They want me back in time for the wedding bells. As soon as I know they'll set the date.' "

"Do you suppose Aunt Julia will have a big wedding?"

"No. It's somewhere here." Her mother flipped through the pages. " 'Julia wants a simple home wedding.' "

"Oh, so Beau and Kim can look on. Isn't it a shame Twilight has to be left out?"

Mrs. Saunders burst into laughter. "I wish your father had been here to get that last."

"Go ahead. Laugh. Just the same, you'll see they won't be barred out. And I think it's going to be one of the nicest weddings I ever heard of."

Her mother's face grew serious. "I'm not sure but what you're right. And one of the happiest."

"And I have to miss it! Well, some vacation soon I've got to visit them."

Mrs. Saunders' eyes twinkled at her. "Get Beau and Kim to arrange it. You seem to think they know how."

Sunny grinned back. "Or Diamond. He's good at fixing things, too."

Diamond! Uncle Joe coming for a visit! What if he came this week and found Ruth the rider?

A clammy fear seized Sunny. Her uncle's warning words rang in her ears. "Different situation at home. School interests interfere. Diamond yours to ride yourself."

Hers to ride. Not Ruth. He had been emphatic that Diamond would continue with her only if she complied. But she wasn't neglecting Diamond, losing interest in him.

Yet the actual facts were that she was not riding him. Her friend was, and the reason given Ruth was that a "school interest," making that village, came first. If Uncle Joe believed that! And he might be arriving any time. Oh, she must not let him find Ruth the rider. She must ride herself in the show.

Carol had come in and Mother was telling her about her aunt's coming marriage. The whole family was excited, and they discussed it all evening. So many wanted to talk at once that nobody noticed Sunny's silence.

She decided to keep still about her private fears, her alarm at her uncle's possible visit. After all, he had set no date, and tomorrow she would fix it so he'd find her in Diamond's saddle. She would take no chances.

Sunny did not know why she did not want to discuss her alarm with the family. She only knew she wanted to see Ruth first, alone. It mattered most to Ruth, and Sunny felt she would never want her to go ahead with it, if it meant she might lose Diamond. Ruth had come to love Diamond, too. She would understand. She would want to step out of the show. But she must talk to her first, alone.

Sunny had never been conscious before of how hard it was to have any privacy around school. Yet she had often talked secrets with friends. This somehow was different. She did not want Ruth's feelings broadcast. Coming out of a clear sky, at the last moment, Ruth would be terribly disappointed.

It was a horrible day. She could not get Ruth off by herself. They came together often. They always ate lunch with each other—and a lot of others. She needed a really alone conversation with her.

The bus going out was so full Sunny and Ruth could not even sit together. Arriving at the Farm, Ruth vanished in the rush of excited soon-to-be riders. Sunny had a tricky hiding place for carrots and got a few for Diamond, but by the time she reached his stall he was gone.

Sunny knew where she could find him. There was a large class scheduled for the outdoor ring. Ruth was probably riding inside. That ring was no place for a private conversation. Sunny wandered aimlessly around the box stalls.

Mr. Cleveland was bringing his mare out of her

stall, and Sunny stopped to admire her. "She gets prettier all the time."

Mr. Cleveland smiled. "You're the girl who rode that black horse with me the other day, aren't you?"

Sunny nodded.

"I'd been hoping we'd meet again. Our horses went well together."

"I haven't been riding much. My friend has been practicing on Diamond."

"Working up for the show Saturday, I take it. All the young folks seem very excited about it."

"Yes." He made it sound harder than ever to tell Ruth she was not to ride.

He noticed that all the animation had left her face.

"You are riding, aren't you?"

"No. Wait, yes, I am. Oh, it is all so terrible."

She walked away from him as fast as she could. In another minute she would be blurting out everything. He seemed like an old friend though she had met him only once. Maybe that was because they liked each other's horses.

His eyes followed her, puzzled, but with a shrug he

let her go and led Gay-Day in the other direction.

Sunny stayed around the stalls a while longer, but looking at other people's horses made her think more and more about the wonder of owning one. Now she might lose Diamond. She must do something.

She went into the glassed-in spectators' stand to see if Ruth was in that ring. There were a number riding, but she picked her out at once. Diamond must be behaving ideally, for as they rode by, Ruth was glowing with enthusiasm and satisfaction.

She had to spoil all that, when she was not even sure when Uncle Joe was coming. But she could not take chances if it meant she might lose Diamond forever. Ruth would not want her to.

Suddenly she saw Mr. Cleveland standing behind her. Later she learned that he had seen her there while he was riding and left Gay-Day tied at a rail to come to talk to her.

"Your black beauty is performing splendidly," he told her.

"Isn't he! It makes it all the worse that Ruth can't ride in the show."

"Why can't she?"

They were alone, and Sunny explained why she must take the horse from her friend.

He listened very attentively. "Perhaps it can be arranged for you both to ride."

"Not with that snide rule of the Horseshoers. If it was just myself having a chance for ribbons I was willing to let her have all the entries. But I had no idea Uncle Joe was coming," she ended in a wail.

"You think he will be here?"

"No. Not so soon. But I can't take the chance."

"I was interested the other day in what you were telling me about quicksand out in Colorado and the way your horse acted, so that a group could trust him to tell if it was safe to cross."

The recollection brought back a smile to Sunny's lips. "Then when he wanted to see what the cloudburst had done that day he took all sorts of chances."

"That is what I was remembering. When he was alone with you. And you were part of him," Mr. Cleveland added.

"That's what's always so wonderful. Being part of

him. Now think of it—if we were separated. Diamond would believe I did not want him any more. And Uncle Joe would not believe I deserved to keep my horse."

Mr. Cleveland had been keenly eying the rider in the ring. "Your friend handles that horse well. Very well. I have to go talk to Colonel Dwyer now. But I hope to be seeing you again—soon."

Sunny said good-bye mechanically. She was thinking about Diamond and his way of taking chances. She had a feeling he knew there was real danger that day he had leaped, trusting to land on ground still solid. He jumped knowing the hazard of quicksand.

The chances of Uncle Joe's arriving were far less than those he had ignored that day. She had been part of him the day he made the decision. Now he was still part of her, and she had to make the decision for them both.

Ruth rode up the last minute. In the hurry of getting into the bus and finding seats, they had no chance for any conversation. Sunny discovered she still had Diamond's carrots in her hand. Ruth left the bus before she could say anything to her.

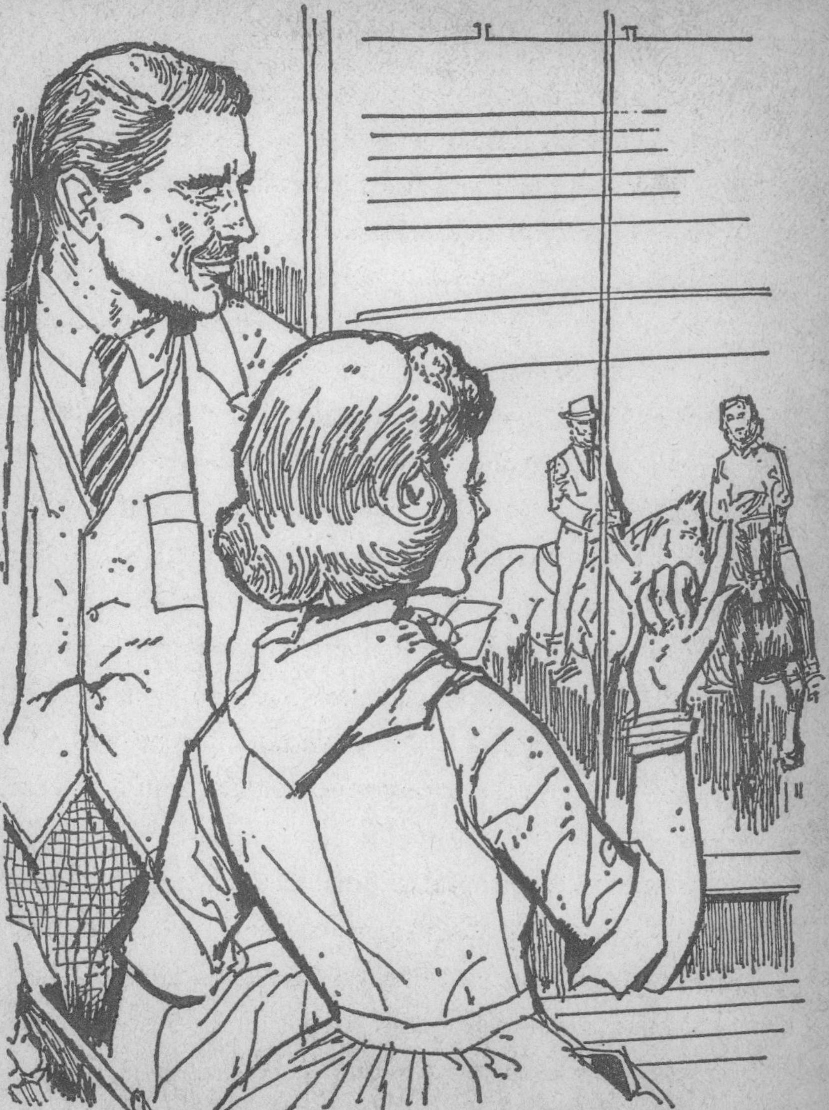

The moment Sunny entered the house, she thought of the telephone. She could call Ruth. If nothing else she could tell her she wanted to talk to her. She could wait until she got her alone to tell her why.

Yet she did not go near the stand. If only she could make up her mind!

She was conscious of her family's efforts at the dinner table to cheer her up. They thought, of course, she was downcast about not riding in the show.

Mrs. Saunders commented, "We ought to be getting busy about a wedding present. If we hurry we might get it there in time."

Mr. Saunders turned to Sunny with a twinkle in his eyes. "What do you suggest we send? You ought to know more about a four-footed wedding than the rest of us."

"You won't believe me but they might be delighted with something for the puppies. A very fancy something."

"You can get something fancy and expensive enough," Mrs. Saunders agreed. "But don't we want something more enduring? Wedding presents are supposed to last for years and years."

"The puppies will, too," Sunny insisted.

"Won't they grow up?" asked Norman.

"Naturally those puppies will. But there will be new ones later. You should have heard them planning."

Mr. Saunders' response was not too enthusiastic. "Is that so? Well, I dare say it can be made a regular business and a profitable one."

"And such fun!" added Sunny, smiling as she thought of how sweet Kim would be with her babies.

Her father eyed her smile with satisfaction. "Look here, Sunny, how about your being the one to select the present?"

Mrs. Saunders objected. "Silver is what is appropriate. Don't let's get carried away and act foolish."

"But Sunny—" Mr. Saunders broke off.

Mrs. Saunders took over smoothly, "Sunny could have a lot of fun buying something, but wedding presents are too serious a business. There will be something else to cheer—that is, for Sunny to have fun with."

All these efforts to make her forget her disappointment did not escape Sunny. And they did not know half of what was getting her down!

She started to tell them. But, no! She knew too well what their advice would be. Yes, what was best for Sunny herself. Deep in her, she knew the decision must be her own. That "best" was so very involved.

Since she had done no work before dinner, the entire dishwashing job was hers, but Carol came out to help. "I haven't a thing to do. Let me wipe."

She did more of the disagreeable stacking than Sunny, whose thoughts kept drifting to the telephone. She must make up her mind. Was she or wasn't she going to call Ruth?

Dishwashing over, she found herself going from room to room, watching the television with Norman, taking its weather reports to her father, checking up on Carol's dressmaking efforts, which were reaching the buttonhole stage. Soon Carol put on the dress, and she helped her pin places for buttons.

For a miracle, the telephone had been silent all evening, yet never had she been more aware of it.

Her mother passed her in the hall and flung her arms

around her. "Oh, Sunny, I wish I had not let you do this for Ruth. I'd no idea it would make you this miserable. But it is doing all you said it would for Ruth. Her mother can't get over the change in her."

It had been on the tip of Sunny's tongue to spill out that she had been on the way to the telephone to change all this. Somehow she didn't. Maybe because Carol called to her mother to know where she could find some blue buttonhole thread.

Instead of going to the telephone, she slipped into her own room and flung herself on her bed. If only she knew what she ought to do—hurt Ruth or risk losing Diamond. She wanted to let go and bawl and bawl, but that would not help anything.

Her mother understood that all this was no neglect of Diamond. But her mother was prejudiced, to say the least. It was not as a prejudiced relative that Uncle Joe had warned her she could have Diamond only as long as she met his terms. Would he understand her motives when all the facts were against her?

She thought of Mr. Cleveland. He was a man, like Uncle, and she was sure he had believed her. Maybe he had reminded her of that quicksand story to let her see she ought to take a chance, that Diamond would.

Yes, she was sure Diamond would, if he were, humanly, to comprehend her choice. If she let Ruth down, she would always, when riding him, know that she had not measured up to his standards. He did not believe in letting people down.

Anyway she would not call Ruth.

She undressed and went to bed. Two more days and Uncle Joe could come safely. After Saturday she was going to have a ride every single day of the week, come what would.

17 *The All-Important Choice*

As Sunny entered her Social Studies class the next morning, Miss Cleeves called her over. "Everybody is admiring your village. Even teachers are coming in to see it. Now it is to have a real honor. Smith's Hardware, the biggest in town, has asked our principal to let them show it. They want to use a whole window for the display—as an example of the fine work done in our schools."

"Honest?" Sunny gasped. "I never thought I'd get an honor like that."

"They're having a handsome sign printed to stand behind it. They had me help with the wording. It's to tell what the model is about, why it was made, and who made it. Your full name."

"But Jean did as much as I did last year. Lots of the ideas were hers."

"That was another model. You did all the work on this one and deserve all the credit. Your name is to be in big print. The class is going to be very proud of you."

As soon as everyone was seated, she told about it. The students clapped and beamed at Sunny. She could never again feel that she had not been a first. Maybe this was no actual piece of silk, but it was a blue ribbon pinned on her work. After class she responded with a glowing face to her classmates' congratulations.

At lunch hour, the news spread around, and she was scarcely given time to eat. Ruth was interrupted again and again when she tried to discuss the plan for getting Diamond to the show.

"Mother wants you to ride him over so I'll be fresher in the afternoon. Do you mind?"

After several interruptions, Sunny assured her she'd enjoy doing it.

After still more interruptions, Ruth told her that her mother would drive her out and pick her up at the other stable, and after still more interruptions, Ruth finished, "She is going over to your house today and plan it all with your mother."

"Anything will be fine with us," Sunny found a chance to tell her.

Sunny knew she had not been doing good work lately, and today she had failed completely to concentrate on lessons. She had been too upset for some time. She had so much to fear now. To lose Diamond!

Soon she realized her teachers thought she was too excited over her new honor to pay proper attention to work, and they were willing to forgive her in these circumstances. Well, Monday she would buckle down to lessons again. She'd better, or her next grades would be a disgrace.

Ruth, Sunny, and a number of other riders were ready for the bus long before it drove up. Everyone but Sunny was worrying about last-minute needs for the show. They must not forget this; they must remember that. Sunny offered to help where she could.

To their surprise, Ruth's mother met them as they stepped out. "Oh, Sunny, we tried to catch you before you left school. Nobody seemed able to. We wanted to bring you out."

"The bus made about the same time," Ruth put in. "Why all the bother?"

Her excited mother laid her hand on Sunny's arm. "Because we have such a grand surprise for you, dear. I was at your house making plans for tomorrow when your uncle's taxi drove up. He was delighted to have me drive him out. I ran into Miss Cleeves yesterday on the street and she told me all about the window display. Your uncle was so interested hearing how wonderful it is that Ruth could take over all your riding so you could do such a fine job."

"You mean Uncle Joe is here now—today?" Nothing worse could have happened than the way it had. The world could as well stop turning.

"He's right here." She looked around in all directions. "He was over there with your mother. Oh, here she comes."

Mrs. Saunders hurried up. She pulled Sunny aside to whisper, "I couldn't say anything. I didn't want to spoil things for them. I'll explain it all to Joe later."

Later. After he had taken in the whole situation and formed his opinion and decided she was more interested in school activities than in her horse. He would learn she was not riding Diamond at all. Exactly as he had said he feared might happen. What use would explanations be? He was getting facts he would believe.

"Where is he?" she faltered.

"Over at Colonel Dwyer's house. It seems he met him years ago when they were in the Army together."

And the Colonel had never been one to believe in her plan for Ruth, to feel it important that Ruth ride. He might even believe that she had cared more about that model of a village. On every side Uncle Joe was hearing how grand it was that her work was being honored so. And her feelings for Diamond? All he'd hear was that she had scarcely ridden him in the last ten days.

If only she could have talked to Uncle Joe first! Before everyone convinced him of something different! Now what hope had she?

She went here and there. She helped the ones she had promised to help. She even went over to the indoor ring to watch Ruth riding Diamond, but she turned quickly away from the sight of them.

She might have been the one on Diamond's back. She had had the unbelievable happiness of being his owner, riding as one with him. She had thrown away her right. Uncle Joe had warned her, had stated the terms in plain English. She had not kept the bargain.

But, she told herself, she had been trying to do what was right, what Diamond would encourage her to do in her place. Still there remained Uncle Joe's terms, to which she had not conformed.

She still had seen no sign of him. The Colonel hurried into the tack room to attend to some rider's need. After several attempts she was able to ask him where her uncle was.

"Over at the house. Here, Bob, you didn't get that entry blank right. We can still fix it, but see we do. Don't get away before it's done."

The Colonel had no more time for her. He had not told her she could go over to his house and find her uncle, and riders were not supposed to go there without a special invitation.

She returned to the lounge. Her mother greeted her, "There's no use trying to arrange anything with

Colonel Dwyer. He's too busy. We can phone tonight. He knows you'll be willing to do the riding, Sunny. Why don't we get Uncle Joe, and you come along home with us? Ruth can use the bus later."

Ruth's mother chimed in, "Has he seen the horse? He was so pleased to hear the good shape he's in. And I do want him to see how beautifully Ruth rides him."

"Is he still over at the house?" questioned Mrs. Saunders.

Sunny answered, "I think so. Alan tells me some of the men riders are over there, too."

"Why don't you go over and find out if he'd rather stay or go home?" suggested her mother.

"It's out of bounds for me."

Neither of the mothers liked the idea of being the one to intrude. "Let's wait till he shows up."

Sunny wondered which was worse, waiting for the blow to fall or riding home listening to a pleased mother tell of Ruth's willingness to be helpful, of how fortunate it all had been.

Fortunate! Could anything have worked out more fiendishly? And instead of doing anything to improve matters, all she could do was stand around and wait.

Alan came into the lounge to get something and she crossed to speak to him again. He told her, "I'm putting in time while my kid brother uses my saddle. Lucky the Horseshoers haven't ruled a saddle can't appear with different riders. Bud has used my saddle before and likes it. Did you know several of the boarders are letting us use their horses? None of the really top ones, but every mount helps. Bud's getting a fair horse."

"Do you know exactly who is over at the house?" Sunny broke in.

"I'm not sure. I think one was the owner of Gay-Day."

"Mr. Cleveland!" cried Sunny, brightening. "Oh, Alan, I think he'd tell Uncle I let Ruth ride because—" She caught herself up and glanced around to be sure Ruth's mother was not overhearing. She went on in a whisper, "Well, not because I'm neglecting my horse."

"Who'd ever think that?"

"Uncle Joe," Sunny replied mournfully.

"You tell him differently."

Her sad eyes studied his face. "Do you think he will believe me?"

"Why not?"

"Look at the facts. I have been paying more attention to that 'school activity' than I have to my horse. Exactly as Uncle Joe said I might. I was to have Diamond only as long as I didn't."

"He'll know this is different," Alan consoled her.

"Will he?" Alan had not seen Uncle Joe's serious face as he stated terms.

Her heart leaped. There he was, coming into the lounge. And walking beside him was Mr. Cleveland, her one hope. But how could she know he remembered what she'd told him? He may have regarded it as mere youngster's foolishness. With her uncle, he may have been talking—oh, politics, grown-up people's talk.

She raced to Uncle Joe and into his arms. For a moment she hugged him tight, then braced back to study his face. Its warmth heartened her. He still loved her, even if he might take Diamond from her. Anyway, he did not wholly disapprove of her.

Colonel Dwyer came hurrying into the lounge and strode toward them. "This offer, Mr. Cleveland, is mighty good of you."

"Don't thank me. Thank the young ladies who deserve it. I feel entirely safe entrusting Gay-Day to either one of them."

Sunny looked from face to face, bewildered. Uncle Joe explained, "Mr. Cleveland has offered to let you ride his mare in the show. I understand good horses are badly needed."

"Are they!" Colonel Dwyer beamed at Mr. Cleveland.

He smiled back. "So I'd been told, but I hardly felt that a kids' show was a place for Gay-Day. However, since I've ridden with Sunny here, and watched her friend faithfully practice hour after hour and seen her show gentleness and real skill in handling a horse, I've changed my mind. I tried to tell you yesterday but couldn't find you."

Sunny held her breath. Would any of this help her keep Diamond? He was saying nothing of what she had told him, the reasons for wanting Ruth to ride.

She recalled his telling her it might be possible for them both to ride, that he would see. He must have had this in mind.

"The entries have to be in soon." Colonel Dwyer was still attending to business. "Which one of the girls will ride Gay-Day?"

Sunny looked beseechingly at Mr. Cleveland. "Would it be all right if Ruth rode her and I had Diamond?" To have this last big day with him!

Then she saw her uncle's expression and realized what her choice had meant in his thinking. "Sunny should ride Diamond," was all he said.

Mr. Cleveland nodded. "I agree. Ruth will enjoy Gay-Day, I am sure."

Ruth's mother was startled. "But she has never been on her. Isn't she a very spirited horse?"

"A very well-trained one," replied her owner. "Ruth will find her easier to ride than almost any other entry."

The Colonel nodded. "Rental horses have so many different riders they get to not caring. There's Ruth now." He called her over and quickly, concisely, told her about the change in horses.

Ruth was frightened. "Truly I'm not that much of a rider. Diamond just makes me look good."

The Colonel admitted ruefully, "I never rated your riding up myself. I thought Sunny was biased because she's your friend. But you have done a fine job lately. Mr. Cleveland has watched you and he would not offer his horse if he did not think you deserved her."

Ruth gulped. "But me! On Gay-Day!"

Sunny seized her hand and squeezed it. "It's true, Ruth. You've got to believe now that you are a real rider."

Mr. Cleveland suggested, "Suppose you take a trial ride on her right now."

"It's so late," Ruth protested. "I'd have no chance to practice on her. The show is tomorrow."

Mr. Cleveland laughed. "You have no need to. Gay-Day is practically a professional in show work. She's been trained in all the tricks that please judges. Merely ride her correctly—as you've shown you know how to do. Leave the rest up to her. Come on. We'll get her in the ring."

As Uncle Joe, Sunny, and the two women moved

toward the glassed-in area so they could watch Ruth, Mrs. Saunders touched Sunny's arm. "How about practice on Diamond? There is so little time before the show."

Sunny was not worried. "Ruth's been getting him in form. Me—it won't be my first ride on him." She stole a glance at Uncle Joe. At last she could talk to him.

The two mothers became intent on watching Ruth enter the ring on Gay-Day. Sunny pulled her uncle around to face her. "Please, won't you believe me? I have never put anything but Diamond first."

"Why, of course not."

"I know you've been hearing all about my not riding —giving all my time to school activities."

"Look here, Sunny, don't you give me credit for any sense? Don't I know that a girl who loves horses as you and I do would never put making an imitation African village ahead of the joy of riding a live horse?"

Sunny flung her arms around him. "Of course no one would. But you see I—"

"Forget it. Watch over there. That is one fine mare

all right. Haw! She's taking her into a great trot."

All four watched with silent delight.

Abruptly, Sunny exclaimed, "That's a funny trot she has now."

Uncle Joe frowned. "It's not a trot. Hey, the horse is racking."

After the mare had completed the ring at this gait, Mr. Cleveland stopped her. Behind the glass they could not hear a word he was saying, but from his motions they knew he was giving Ruth detailed instructions.

Ruth walked her horse away, then put her into a true trot. He stopped her once again. Then Ruth made the horse rack for her. After another trot around the ring, he motioned to her and she headed Gay-Day for the gate.

When Ruth rejoined them, she was bubbling with enthusiasm. "All you have to do is sit on her. She scarcely jiggles you."

Sunny laughed. "Easier to ride than that Torchy who dumped you, isn't she? But, Ruth, don't forget horses like Gay-Day *give* for a good rider. They are a

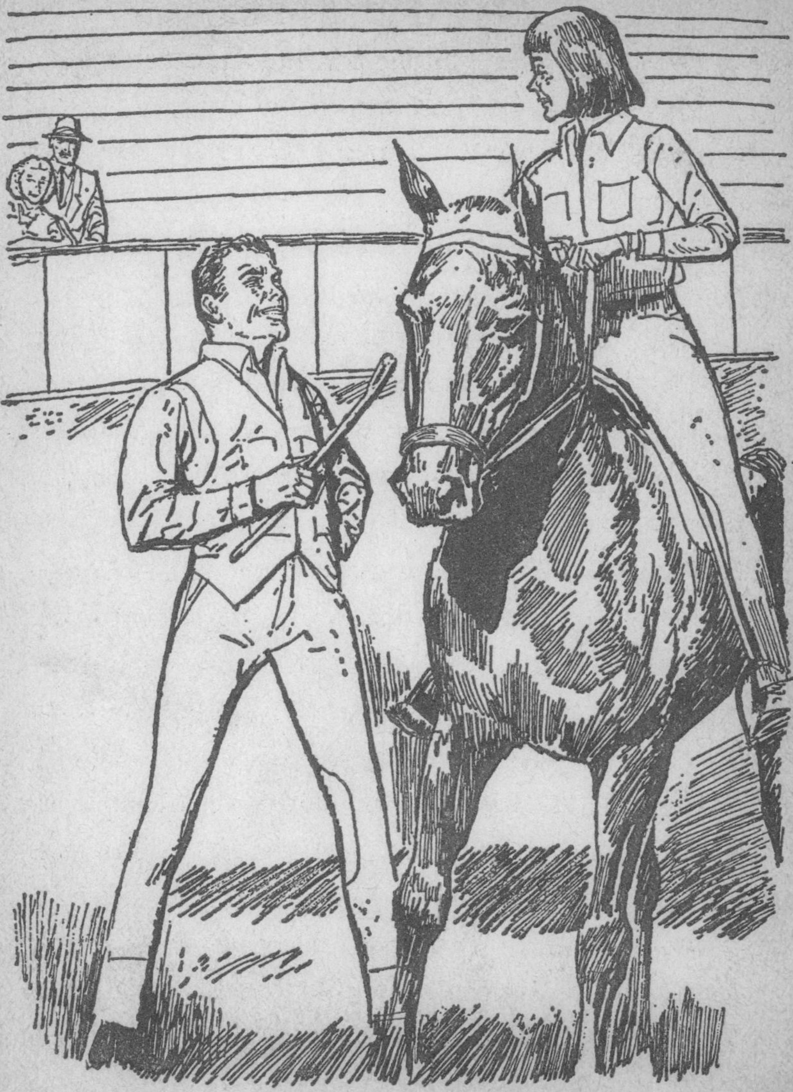

lot more discriminating than Torchy. And Mr. Cleveland put you on Gay-Day because he believes you can ride."

Driving home, they occasionally changed the subject from horses, but not often. However, Mrs. Saunders, who had some of her curiosity about affairs in Denver answered on the drive out, was still full of questions.

"The wedding will be Tuesday," Uncle Joe explained for Sunny's benefit. "I must be back in Chicago Sunday night. My man was out of town for the weekend so I was able to come here. I can take in the show and leave early Sunday. Then I fly home Monday night. So I'll be on hand for the wedding."

Sunny got in a question. "They are going to let Beau and Kim see them married, aren't they?"

"They are the only guests invited. John Carlton has no family. As they say, they are not romantic youngsters wanting a lot of frills. But, Sis," he turned to Mrs. Saunders, "they are devoted to each other. They are really companionable. They enjoy being with each other."

Mrs. Saunders tried to tease him. "Joe! You sound

almost jealous." She laughed.

He answered seriously, "Maybe I am. Even Beau is neglecting me for Kim's puppies. You should see him with them all over him. Once he didn't even hear me come home. But he made up afterward. Still, I believe you've been right. I have stayed around home too much for years. I am going to start accepting more of the invitations I get where there will be others my age. I'm free to now."

Mrs. Saunders nodded. "For the first time you are. But with Mother—will it last? Will they stay happy— two families—you know how that goes with two under one roof."

"Three! You forgot Kim's puppies. They don't. Even *Mere* Odette thinks their comfort is more important than her French touches. You'd be surprised the changes we've made. I bought some real man chairs. Kim gets to sit in them more than I do. That's all right. I got them into the house and I'll find something Kim likes better."

"I wish I was there to help you," sighed Sunny. "It must be so awfully much fun."

"You make it sound crazy," objected Mrs. Saunders.

"It may be," he agreed readily, "but Julia's happiness isn't. Or the way John Carlton is fitting in. The god of luck was on my side the day I picked his favorite breed of dogs. But then, Kim has ways that win everybody."

"Even Mother!" Mrs. Saunders gave a deep sigh. "I never thought to see her willing to yield the center of attention."

"You forget how much older and frailer she is. Fortunately, it is working so she can stay home in her rocking chair by the fire and rarely be left alone."

"Doesn't Kim want to use the cushion in that rocker?" asked Sunny.

Uncle Joe grinned back at her. "I'm happy to report that Kim prefers stationary chairs—like mine. So *Mere* Odette keeps her own rocker."

Joy sang in Sunny. Everybody was keeping what he wanted and she was keeping Diamond. The sun shone again. The world revolved properly again in its rightful orbit. All was well.

18   *The Real Winner*

The girls were to ride both horses over to the show grounds. Mr. Cleveland preferred not to have Gay-Day put in a trailer or led by a rope. Ruth's mother brought them out early, and they were surprised to see Mr. Cleveland waiting for them.

He greeted the girls, saying, "I never thought about your not knowing Gay-Day is five-gaited. Walk, trot, canter, rack, and slow-gait. I got to thinking later and I want to give you some more instruction," he told Ruth.

He took her into the ring and worked with her until Ruth was sure about changing gaits. While Sunny waited around, she learned that arrangements had been made for grooms to ride the horses home after the show. She was pleased, for it gave her more time with Uncle Joe. The show was taking her away from him too much. It was over an hour before the two girls rode out.

Sunny eyed Gay-Day's high-stepping. "I'm glad it was not Diamond who had to go through all that workout before going over to the show."

"Gay-Day is a lot younger. She's loving it," replied Ruth. "I'm glad we're riding for it gives me more time to be sure I know how to keep her in a trot—and change right."

"Use all her gaits so you can tell the difference," urged Sunny. "A little workout will do Diamond good."

So Ruth went from gait to gait, glowing with delight. Both girls were sorry to reach their destination. Mr. Cleveland had made a special reservation for the use of two box stalls, and the horses were led into them.

Ruth's mother was waiting in her car. Ruth sighed, "I hate to go home. I wish it was afternoon."

"I want to get home to Uncle Joe. He has so much more to tell me. Moms and Dad monopolized him all last evening."

But when she had him alone, she found she knew nearly everything. Beau was fine. Kim, at first, had been a little jealous of his taking the puppies' attention from her, but she had soon seen that he knew how to take care of them. Their rough play did not maul him as it did her. More and more she was inclined to sit back, rest, and let him care for them, except at meal times. They were hungry puppies and already needed extra feedings by the bottle. Mr. Carlton had insisted Aunt Julia try to teach them to lap up their own, but they preferred her bottles.

Uncle Joe admitted the pups were fun. "Cute little duffers. One girl and two boys."

"Exactly right. Uncle Joe, aren't you glad we're living?"

He laughed at her. "Time you were dressed. I heard Colonel Dwyer telling you to report in a little bit early."

Sunny's face sobered for a minute. "I do hope Ruth manages Gay-Day all right."

"How about your managing Diamond? It's your first show with him."

Yes, it was. "But Diamond! I don't have to worry." She said that at home.

The show was held in an outdoor ring. The entries for the first event lined up at one gate. Not a horse was behaving. Even Diamond was dancing around. Maybe it was not going to be so easy. She did not feel at all sure of herself now.

The gate was opened. They were to walk around the ring once, then line up for inspection. The scoring was to be on horsemanship, the rider's performance, but appearance would count one point. Ruth's mother had bought her a handsome new navy-blue suit, and Sunny's had been cleaned.

Once the horses were inside, in motion, they steadied to even walks. One or two gave an occasional prance, which meant a score against them.

The call came to line up. Diamond stretched out beautifully and held it. Sunny tried to have her own posture as good. She wondered if horses minded keeping legs spread as much as she did keeping her back straight. The judges could not have been slower.

At last the call came to walk around the ring, soon

to trot, to stop, to reverse, to walk, canter, trot, stop, walk, canter. On and on, though actually it took only a few minutes. Those managing the show kept it moving rapidly.

"Line up."

There was a brief pause while the judges conferred. Four horses were put back in action, Diamond included. A few more rounds and another line-up. The judges nodded to each other and the ribbons were presented. Sunny gazed enraptured at hers. Red! Incredible with the number of entries she had been up against.

The next event was for a younger age. A Timber Trail Rider won a ribbon.

There had been too many entries for some numbers. The first event had been split into two groups, by drawing. The second group was entering the ring. Ruth's turn had come.

Sunny had known twinges of panic when she herself lined up at the gate, but now with Ruth there panic engulfed her. She would be the one responsible if Ruth failed and was made a hundred times more unhappy than if she had given up riding as she had intended doing. Sunny had pushed Ruth into this. That five-gaited horse could do anything.

The mare did exactly what her owner had predicted, gave a thoroughly professional performance. Ruth was never flurried, never diverted from riding form.

After the second line-up, three horses were sent again around the ring. Gay-Day was not one. Sunny's heart sank.

The horses again lined up. The judges conferred, plainly discussing the three who had just repeated. Finally a decision was reached, and the ribbons were handed out. As a matter of course the blue one was handed to Ruth. There had been no debate about that award.

Sunny discovered tears were stinging her eyes. The struggle to make Ruth a rider was over. The two of them had happy riding days ahead.

They were shouting for her to hurry up. The line was already formed for the trick number. Each rider carried an egg in a spoon and held it well extended. Egg after egg bounced off. A Horseshoe rider on a

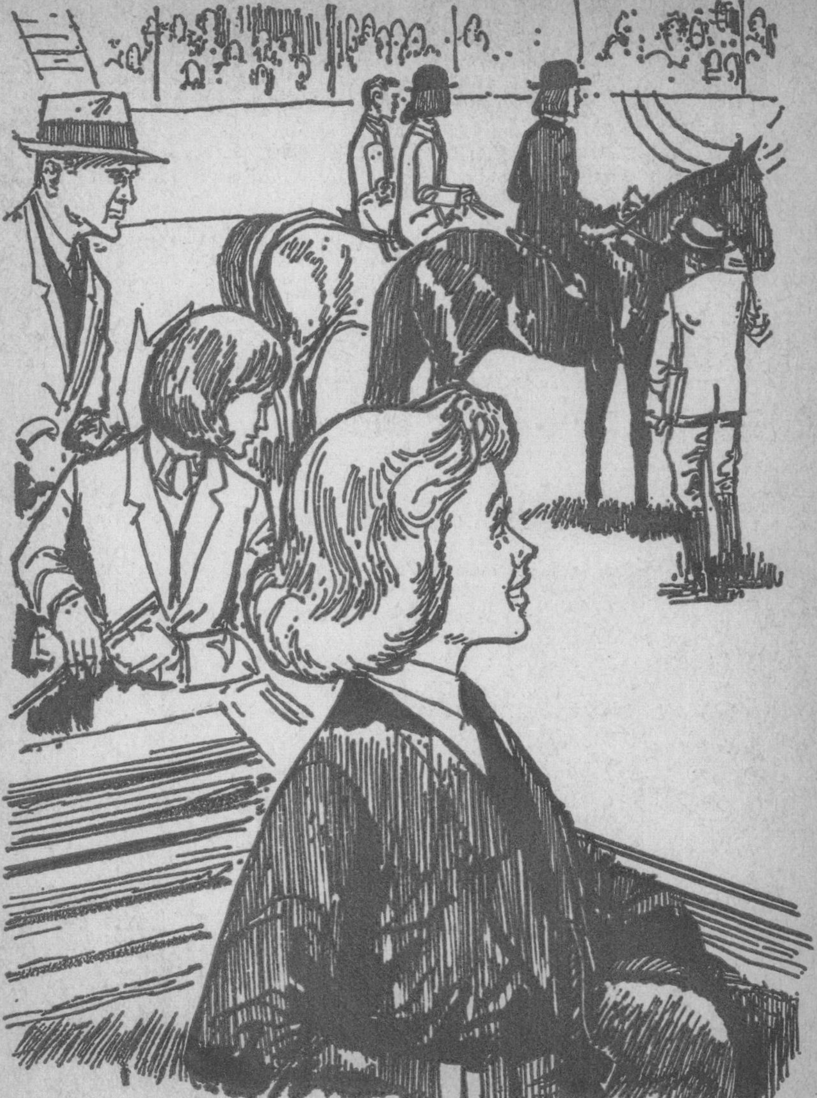

racking horse gave the showiest performance.

The judges called, "Now all horses trot." The Horseshoe rider's egg jolted off almost at once.

Sunny won a blue ribbon.

The next event was a barrel stunt, not exactly a race though speed counted more than form. No horse or rider could touch a barrel. Rider after rider was ruled out for that. The blue ribbon went to a tomboy, who owned a horse, kept at a private stable, and was used to rowdy riding.

Diamond performed well, but he was a shade too careful of his bones, and Sunny did not urge him. They failed to place. Ruth trailed with the poorest. She did not even try. Two Timber Trail Riders did win.

At the last minute, the Horseshoe Club had added another number, for five-gaited horses. They expected to have all the entries. Instead Ruth walked off with another blue ribbon, eight points, while the other three brought in only seven.

Sunny noticed something. She had heard the judges did not like the one-rider rule but they had no power to change it. All three were being scrupulously fair, but they were not letting a single slip made by the Horseshoe riders escape them. The club was winning ribbons but it was not walking away with the show.

Several Timber Trail Riders won in younger classes. Alan won a red in musical chairs. Ruth was so afraid Gay-Day would get hurt that she kept her practically on the sidelines. Sunny was nearly as bad, for she did not like jostling horses any more than Diamond did. Neither won anything.

As it grew late, they hurried numbers all they could. The final entries lined up almost on schedule. The blue ribbon winners of every class were to compete with each other.

From the beginning, it was clear the contest was to be between Ruth, Sunny, the winner of the first event, and a rider from the Horseshoe Club on a fine mare. She had lost before to Ruth, but she won a blue in another event and was qualified for this final judging.

Very soon the other riders were lined up in the center, and the proud four rode the ring. Never had Diamond stepped out better. Never had Sunny loved him more for it. He was not a high-stepper, like some, but he made motion beautiful. He was *all* horse.

And her horse! The joy of the world was riding him, here or anywhere. She almost forgot they were riding for a ribbon. And they rode superbly.

Sunny learned later that Ruth slipped once, breaking her horse into a rack. Ruth always insisted it was a mistake. If she had done it on purpose wouldn't she have chanced a Horseshoer winning? How could she know Sunny would if she didn't?

The Horseshoe rider tried too hard to show off. She worried her horse and played him down. The fourth rider did well and won a red, but Sunny rode out of the ring carrying a blue ribbon.

As president of the Timber Trail Riders, Pete was presented with the handsome trophy all the clubs had so coveted. He gave Sunny a very special wink as he walked to the center of the ring. The lounge at the Farm would always be a little grander for displaying it.

Uncle Joe met her at the gate. She gave him no chance to congratulate her. As quickly as she could dismount, she pinned the blue ribbon on him.

"Where it belongs," she whispered.

Whitman CLASSICS

Five Little Peppers Midway

Freckles

Wild Animals I Have Known

Rebecca of Sunnybrook Farm

Alice in Wonderland

Mrs. Wiggs of the Cabbage Patch

Fifty Famous Fairy Tales

Rose in Bloom

Eight Cousins

Little Women

Little Men

Five Little Peppers and How They Grew

Robinson Crusoe

Treasure Island

Heidi

The Call of the Wild

Tom Sawyer

Beautiful Joe

Adventures of Sherlock Holmes

Here are some of the best-loved stories of all time. Delightful ... intriguing ... never-to-be-forgotten tales that you will read again and again. Start your own home library of WHITMAN CLASSICS so that you'll always have exciting books at your finger tips.

Whitman
REG. U.S. PAT. OFF.

Whitman ADVENTURE and MYSTERY Books

Adventure Stories for GIRLS and BOYS...

TIMBER TRAIL RIDERS
 The Long Trail North
 The Texas Tenderfoot
 The Luck of Black Diamond

THE BOBBSEY TWINS
 In the Country
 Merry Days Indoors and Out
 At the Seashore

DONNA PARKER
 In Hollywood
 At Cherrydale
 Special Agent
 On Her Own
 A Spring to Remember
 Mystery at Arawak

TROY NESBIT SERIES
 The Forest Fire Mystery
 The Jinx of Payrock Canyon
 Sand Dune Pony

New Stories About Your Television Favorites...

Dr. Kildare
 Assigned to Trouble

Janet Lennon
 And the Angels
 Adventure at Two Rivers
 Camp Calamity

Walt Disney's Annette
 The Mystery at Smugglers' Cove
 The Desert Inn Mystery
 Sierra Summer
 The Mystery at Moonstone Bay

The Lennon Sisters
 Secret of Holiday Island

Leave It to Beaver

Ripcord

The Beverly Hillbillies

Lassie
 The Mystery at Blackberry Bog

Lucy
 The Madcap Mystery